WATTERS · LEYH · DOZERDRAWS · LAIHO

LUMBERJANES™

X MARKS THE SPOT

BOOM!
BOX™

BOOM! BOX™

LUMBERJANES Volume Fourteen, May 2020. Published by BOOM! Box, a division of Boom Entertainment, Inc. Lumberjanes is ™ & © 2020 Shannon Watters, Grace Ellis, Noelle Stevenson & Brooklyn Allen. Originally published in single magazine form as LUMBERJANES No. 53-56. ™ & © 2018 Shannon Watters, Grace Ellis, Noelle Stevenson & Brooklyn Allen. All rights reserved. BOOM! Box™ and the BOOM! Box logo are trademarks of Boom Entertainment, Inc., registered in various countries and categories. All characters, events, and institutions depicted herein are fictional. Any similarity between any of the names, characters, persons, events, and/or institutions in this publication to actual names, characters, and persons, whether living or dead, events, and/or institutions is unintended and purely coincidental. BOOM! Box does not read or accept unsolicited submissions of ideas, stories, or artwork.

For information regarding the CPSIA on this printed material, call: (203) 595-3636 and provide reference #RICH – 885122.

BOOM! Studios, 5670 Wilshire Boulevard, Suite 400, Los Angeles, CA 90036-5679. Printed in USA. First Printing.

ISBN: 978-1-68415-550-7, eISBN: 978-1-64144-716-4

THIS LUMBERJANES FIELD MANUAL BELONGS TO:

NAME:_____

TROOP:_____

DATE INVESTED:_____

FIELD MANUAL TABLE OF CONTENTS

LUMBERJANES
FIELD MANUAL

For the Intermediate Program

Tenth Edition • February 1985

Prepared for the

Miss Qiunzella Thiskwin
Penniquiqul Thistle Crumpet's

CAMP FOR  HARDCORE
LADY-TYPES

"Friendship to the Max!"

A MESSAGE FROM THE LUMBERJANES HIGH COUNCIL

The thing about a good mood is: it is like a balloon. Sometimes they may seem to come from nowhere, surprising you with how much they lift your spirits and warm your heart. At other times, you might blow up several dozen, specifically for a special event or a party, and they will wilt by the end of the evening. Sometimes, you must put a lot of effort into cultivating them, if you would like to have a bright and colorful bouquet to choose from, but other times, a friend may appear and gift you one of theirs.

They are commonplace and pedestrian, but they are also precious and difficult to come by. They can often float far beyond our wildest dreams, but they are also impossibly fragile.

They are ephemeral. Like the first warm breeze of spring, the last bites of an ice cream cone, the long-stretching moments of dreamy half-sleep, before the start of a new day. These are times that cannot last, ways of living and breathing that are only for this moment, and only for you. You can share them, and you can treasure them, but they will still end and leave you only with memories, like perfectly formed pearls.

Protect your good moods and your happy times. Keep them close to you, because they will help you endure difficult days. They will be a raft to keep your head above the surface of stormy seas, or a hot air balloon to carry you, safe and sound, high above the squall below.

THE LUMBERJANES PLEDGE

I solemnly swear to do my best
Every day, and in all that I do,
To be brave and strong,
To be truthful and compassionate,
To be interesting and interested,
To pay attention and question
The world around me,
To think of others first,
To always help and protect my friends,
~~*To respect the spirits and faith in God...*~~

And to make the world a better place
For Lumberjane scouts
And for everyone else.

THEN THERE'S A LINE ABOUT GOD, OR WHATEVER

LUMBERJANES™

X MARKS THE SPOT

Written by
Shannon Watters & Kat Leyh

Illustrated by
Dozerdraws

Colors by
Maarta Laiho

Letters by
Aubrey Aiese

Cover by
Kat Leyh

Designer
Marie Krupina
Series Editor
Dafna Pleban
Collection Editor
Sophie Philips-Roberts
Collection Executive Editor
Jeanine Schaefer
*Special thanks to **Kelsey Pate** for giving the Lumberjanes their name.*

Created by **Shannon Watters, Grace Ellis, Noelle Stevenson & Brooklyn Allen**

LUMBERJANES FIELD MANUAL

CHAPTER
FIFTY-THREE

Is there ANY sign of it?

ROANOKE

It's gotta be around here somewhere!

I mean, it must be, right?

How does anyone lose something that's neon orange?

Didn't you hang it up after the last time we went swimming?

Definitely! Probably! Maybe?

Oh, Ripley... it's gonna STINK!

Oo!

Did you find it?

I found my candy stash! I thought the yetis took it!

Sigh

mm-hm!

We're gonna go wait outside! Come on out when you find your swimsuit!

Ooo! Stickers!

GAAASP

ROANOKE

guysguysguysguysguys!

Did you find your--

BETTER, MAL!

It's a...map?

Is that the scroll Barney gave us a while ago? I *wondered* where that went!

YEAH, JO! A TREASURE MAP!

It's for around here! There's the lighthouse!

I thought it got swallowed up by the trash monster!

April, don't joke about that, it could be a real thing.

Why is there more than one X?

GASP

MORE THAN ONE TREASURE...

We're doing this, right? We're gonna find the treasure?

HECKS TO THE YES WE ARE!

Oh, thank GOODNESS we're not swimming, yes.

Jo?

OBVIOUSLY we're going treasure hunting!

First of all, we're going to need to find some landmarks...

If we can't do that, this and ANY map will be useless.

Nooo.

We need more than one reference point to establish--

The butt!

It's a butte...

But I think you're right!

And THAT means...

Let's see, I have the distance from camp to the mountain...

...camp to the lighthouse...

...triangulate ...if I can...

I'VE GOT IT! A mile is 2.38 inches! The closest X is this way!

Come on!

YEAH YEAH YEAH, THAT'S MY GIRL! CALCULATE THAT RELATIVE DISTANCE!

We're close!

So what do you think the treasure's going to be?

Hmm...I mean, the map seems so old! Whatever we're looking for is going to be ANCIENT! Maybe something we could bring to a museum!

Very old-stuff nerdy of you, Molly, I like it!

I'M imagining like, FIVE to EIGHT treasure chests! Like a prolific pirate had more treasure than only one spot could POSSIBLY hold!

A classic, excellent choice. Very "children's menu at a family restaurant" of you, April.

Thank you, Molly.

What if it's like, five pieces of ANOTHER map that you have to reassemble and THAT map leads to an even MORE amazing treasure?!

Is that what YOU would do if you made a treasure map?

Yup!

What do you think, Jo?

I'm thinking it's GOT to be something magic, right? Something like the different pieces of the same...wish-granting amulet or something...

Yeaaah! Why haven't we found anything like **that** yet?

I bet we're about to!

What do you think, Rip?

Yeah, I think it's gonna be all of that for sure for sure. Treasure...MAGIC treasure! Super old magic pirate treasure! And dinosaur bones, I hope...and POSSIBLY snacks? MAGIC DINOSAUR SNACKS???

Probably not snacks.

And it was all buried by super-smart pirate critters!

Okay, okay. I can't ignore this anymore. Is NO ONE going to say anything about this?!

...What?

Hahaha, Ripley, WHY have you been walking on your hands for the last 15 minutes?!

hahaha

I wanted to see if I could! It's fun

Maybe take it easy with all that candy, Rip. You have got an excess of sugar fuel.

Speaking of your candy...

CANDYYYY! NOOOO!

Hey, everybody!

I think we're here! This is it! The first "X"!

Fan out! Start searching!

I'M GONNA START DIGGING!

This...isn't... working...

Gotta take this serious!--

WHOOP!

ow

GASP!

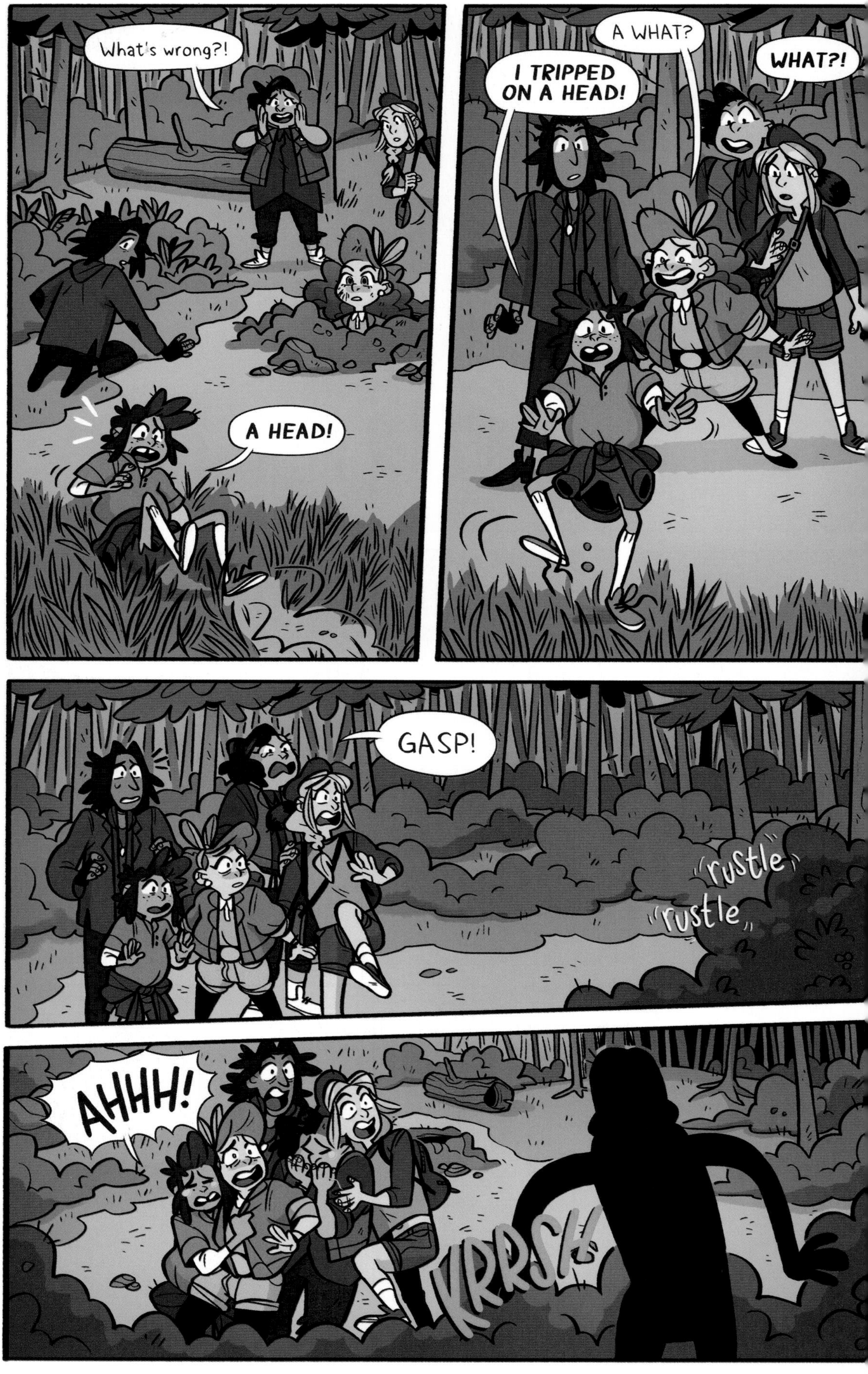
What's wrong?!
A HEAD!
I TRIPPED ON A HEAD!
A WHAT?
WHAT?!
GASP!
rustle
rustle
AHHH!
KRRSH!

AAH--

AH!

--oh

Thank Emmy Noether, it's just Jen!

That's right! Ol' "Just Jen" who has been WAITING for all of you to show up at the lake for the last HALF HOUR, no big deal!

Oops...

How did you FIND us?

I followed... signs of Ripley.

What have you all been doing?!

We're so sorry, Jen! We got caught up!

Yeah! We were looking for my swimsuit...and, well...

Looking for Ripley's swimsuit with a...

...treasure map.

No, no! Ripley FOUND the map when she was looking for her swimsuit, and now we're on a treasure hunt!

Because TREASURE HUNT!

AND we just found--

AH! RIPLEY SAID SHE FOUND A HEAD.

A WHAT?!

Oh, THAT kind of head.

This must be he treasure! Wow!

The treasure is...

...A boring old bit of a STATUE?

I guess Molly got it right!

Yeah! It must be CENTURIES old!

Let's keep look--

The next spot isn't too far from here...

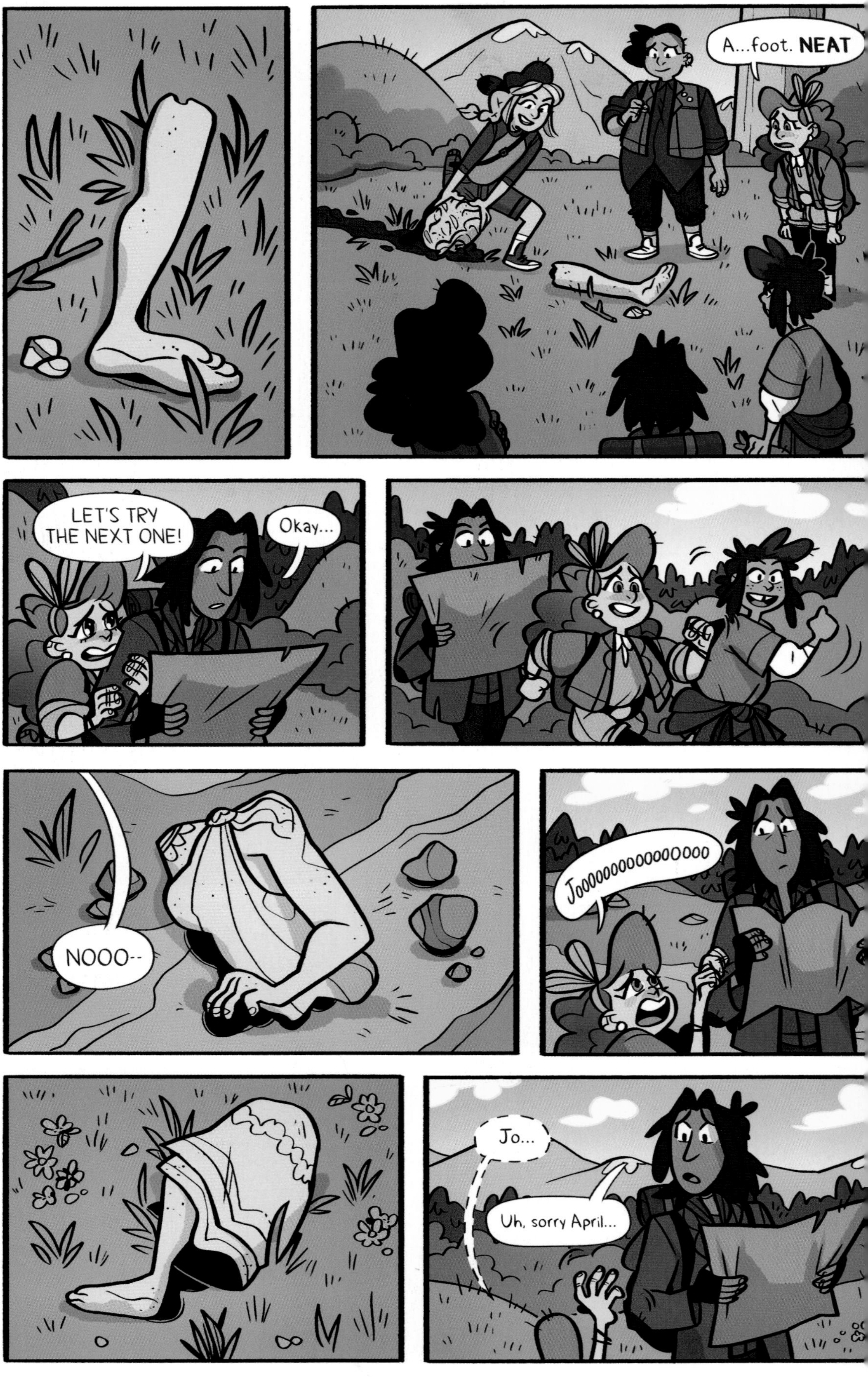
A...foot. NEAT
LET'S TRY THE NEXT ONE!
Okay...
NOOO--
Jooooooooooooooooo
Jo...
Uh, sorry April...

...This is the last X. No more treasure.

NOOOO

This must be all the pieces... what if we put it back together?

Like a craft project!

I wonder if there's a badge for that...

The repaired statues I've seen in museums have these metal bits to hold them together--

I've got this!

A Lumberjane is always prepared!

Ripley, that's not...you shouldn't use...I don't think that'll hold it together...

History...

I use glitter glue for EVERYTHING, it'll hold!

clunk!

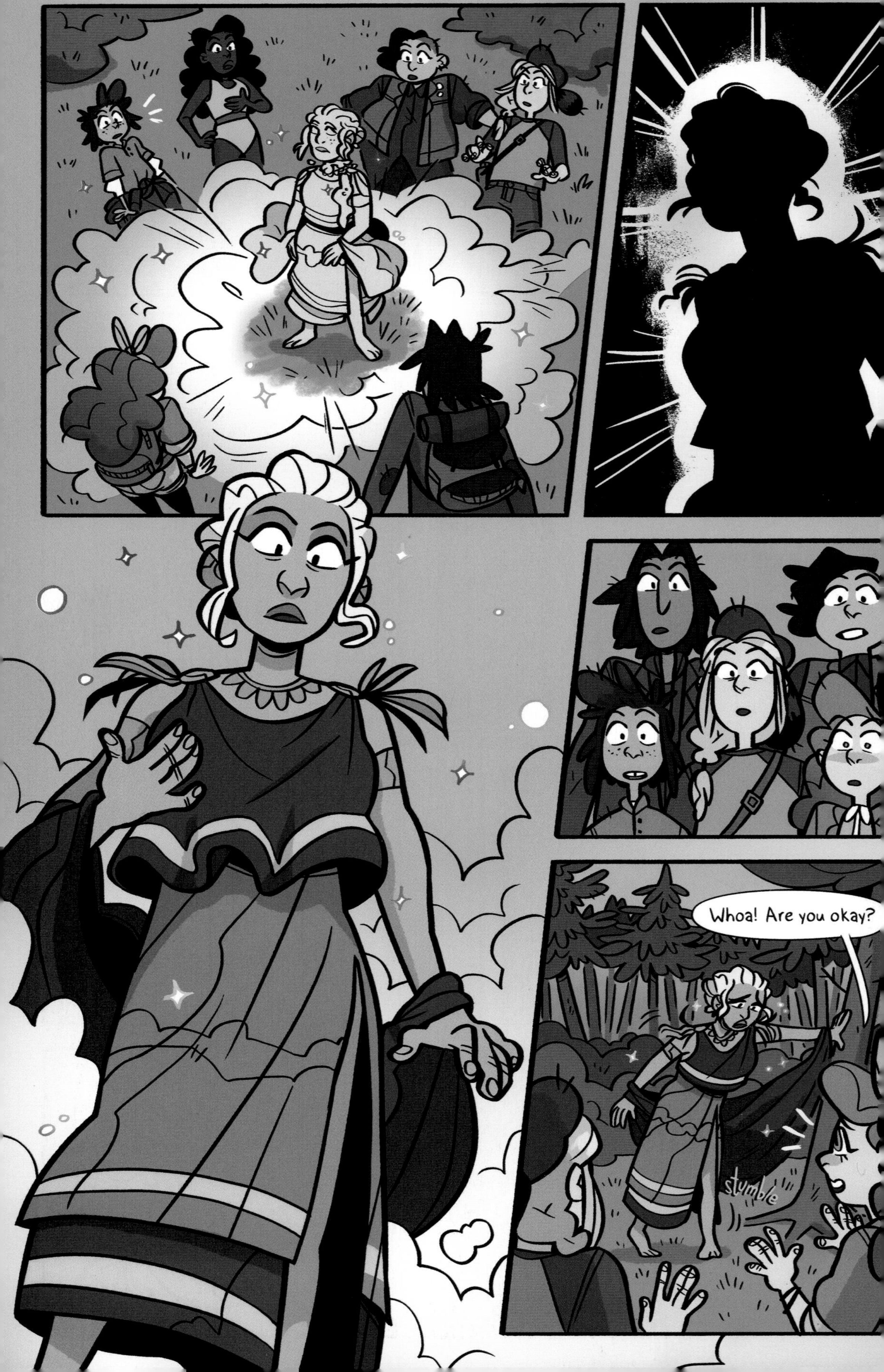
Whoa! Are you okay?
stumble

...What...what has happened?

Uuuh, our friend glued you back together?

You were a statue! But you were scattered all around, so we found all your pieces, and then I glued you back together, and I KNEW my glue would work, but not THIS WELL--

Statue?

What do you remember?

I...it is all a bit fuzzy. You say I was turned to stone?

Yeaaaah, and you look like the old Greek statues at museums and stuff...

Gee, who does all THAT remind you of.

Let's find out if DIANE knows anything about this...

Our cabin's that way! This is the Mess Hall where we eat all our meals... are you hungry?

Rosie's cabin and the moose stables are down that path...you'll meet her at some point...

And over there are the showers... do you need to use the bathroom? Were you like...holding it the whole time you were frozen in stone?

Mal, shush!

ROANOKE

You are all taking this rather well. Is it not strange to you I was a statue?

Let's just say you aren't the FIRST person we've met who's been turned to stone! Or even the fifth!

Oh, my! What strange lives you must lead!

HA! That's **NOTHING!** We have legit battled ACTUAL monsters! And WON!

We're friends with a Gorgon! And yetis! And a werewolf! And PUNK ROCK MERMAIDS!

We got to go to dinosaur times! I got to RIDE DINOSAURS! AND MOTHRA!

We saved Rosie that one time from a giant bird who accidentally kidnapped her.

Lightning bugs, selkies, ghost ponies, giant rock monster, talking fox who's a jerk...

And we can't forget...

...that one time Ripley was given unlimited cosmic god powers and used them to make a bunch of kittens!

And a hat for Bubbles!

AND a hat for Bubbles!

My...goodness!

Speaking of...

Barney! Diane! Just the 'Janes we were looking for!

Oh?

We have a situation that's... well...

It's got a little ancient Greek Goddess hijinks vibe goin' on.

Psh

A Greek Goddess?!

Yeah! Her name's Artemis! And also Diane!

Diane, do you know this woman?

She used to be FROZEN IN STONE if that helps.

Never seen her before.

Are you sure? She's looks straight out of 300 BCE Greece, and we thought--

Hey! It's not like you know, like, every... every person with a raccoon hat!

You're right, sorry...

Excuse me?! You DO always have SOMETHING to do with people getting frozen in stone!

UGH! Get OVER it, already!

So you got a NAME, rock lady?

Yes, Artemis.

Tromatikós.

What the JUNK was that?!

Where is she?! Did she leave?!

...Yeah... she's gone...

Who WAS that? Another goddess?

YOU DON'T KNOW?! You brought that...THING here, and YOU DON'T KNOW?!

SO TELL US!

Hold on...

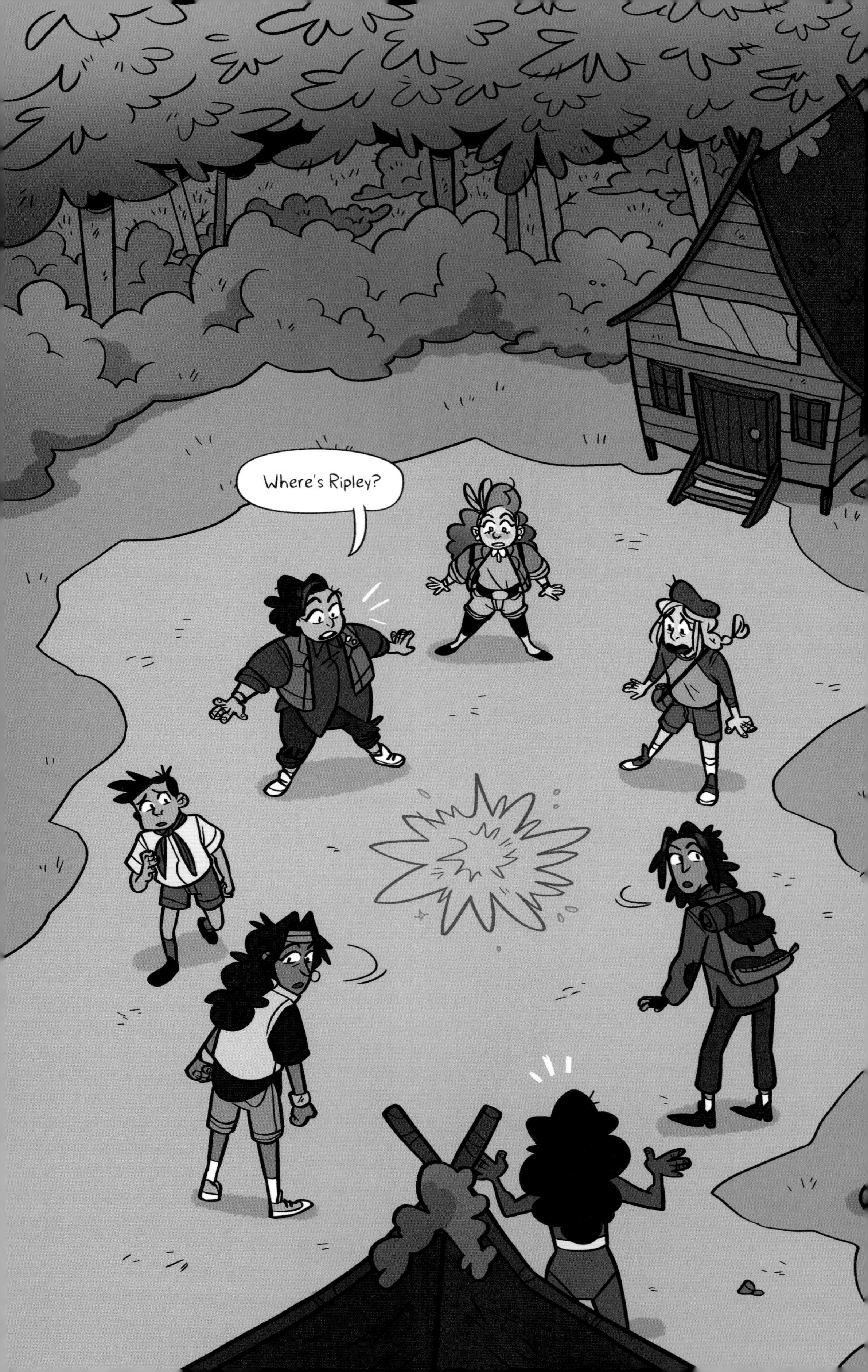
Where's Ripley?

will co...

The u...
It help...
appearan...
dress fo...
Further...
Lumber...
to have...
part in...
Thiskw...
Hardco...
have...
them...

The...
yellow, short sl...
emb...
the w...
choose...
slacks,...
made o...
out-of-do...
green bere...
the colla...
Shoes may...
heels, roun...
socks should...
the uniform. Ne... ...es, bracelets, or other jewelry do...
belong with a Lumberjane uniform.

HOW TO WEAR THE UNIFORM

To look well in a uniform demands first of...
uniform be kept in good condition—clean...
pressed. See that the skirt is the right length for your own
height and build, that the belt is adjusted to your waist,
that your shoes and stockings are in keeping with the
uniform, that you watch your posture and carry yourself
with dignity and grace. If the beret is removed indoors,
be sure that your hair is neat and kept in place with an
inconspicuous clip or ribbon. When you wear a
Lumberjane uniform you are identified as a member of
this organization and you should be doubly careful to
conduct yourself in a way that will show everyone that
courtesy and thoughtfulness are part of being a
Lumberjane. People are likely to judge a whole nation by
the selfishness of a few individuals, to criticize a whole
family because of the misconduct of one member, and to
feel unkindly toward an organization because of the

THE UNIFORM

...should be worn at camp
...events when Lumberjanes
...may also be worn at other
...ions. It should be worn as a
...the uniform dress with
...rect shoes, and stocking or
...out grows her uniform or
...ther Lumberjane.
...a she has
...her
...her

The unif...
helps to cre...
in a group...
active life th...
another bond...
future, and pr...
in order to b...
Lumberjane pr...
Penniquiqul Thi...
Types, but m... ...s will wish to have one. They
can either bu... ... uniform, or make it themselves from
materials available at the trading post.

LUMBERJANES FIELD MANUAL

CHAPTER FIFTY-FOUR

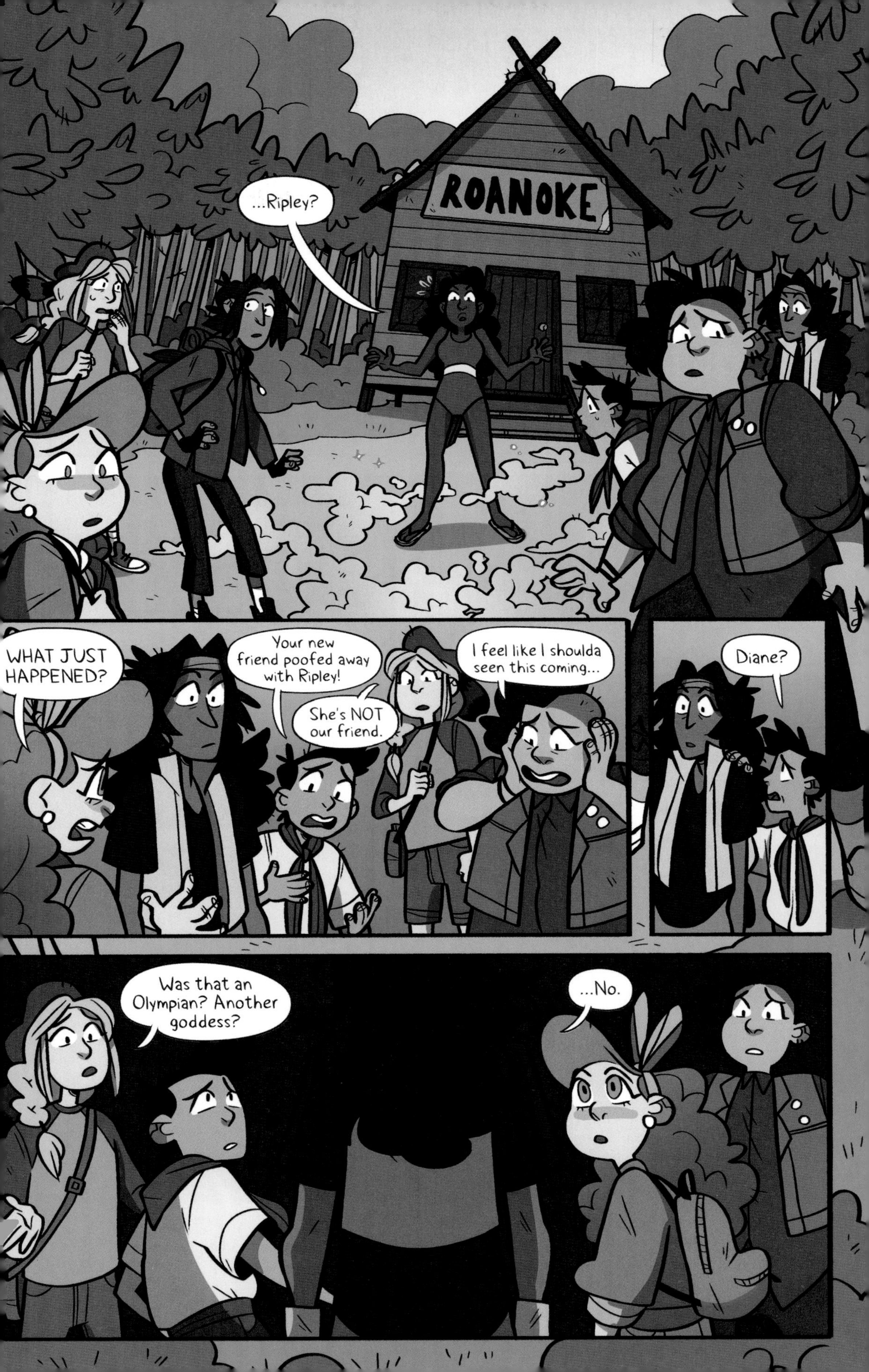
ROANOKE
...Ripley?
WHAT JUST HAPPENED?
Your new friend poofed away with Ripley!
She's NOT our friend.
I feel like I shoulda seen this coming...
Diane?
Was that an Olympian? Another goddess?
...No.

No. She isn't one of ours.

Could you, by chance...elaborate?

It...was before my time.

You called her... Tromatikós? Doesn't that mean--

Tremendous, terrific, terrifying...

...SCARY, APPALLING...

...TRAUMATIC! IT MEANS LOTS OF UNPLEASANT STUFF!

I'm getting Rosie.

All of you STAY. PUT. 'til I get back!

I mean it.

Could you... tell us more, Diane, please?

sigh

These were the EARLY days, before even Apollo and I were born, but I've heard the stories. Apparently...one day...she just...

"...showed up.

...one knew where she came from... ...ich was odd 'cause the gods were supposed to know everything.

"However..."

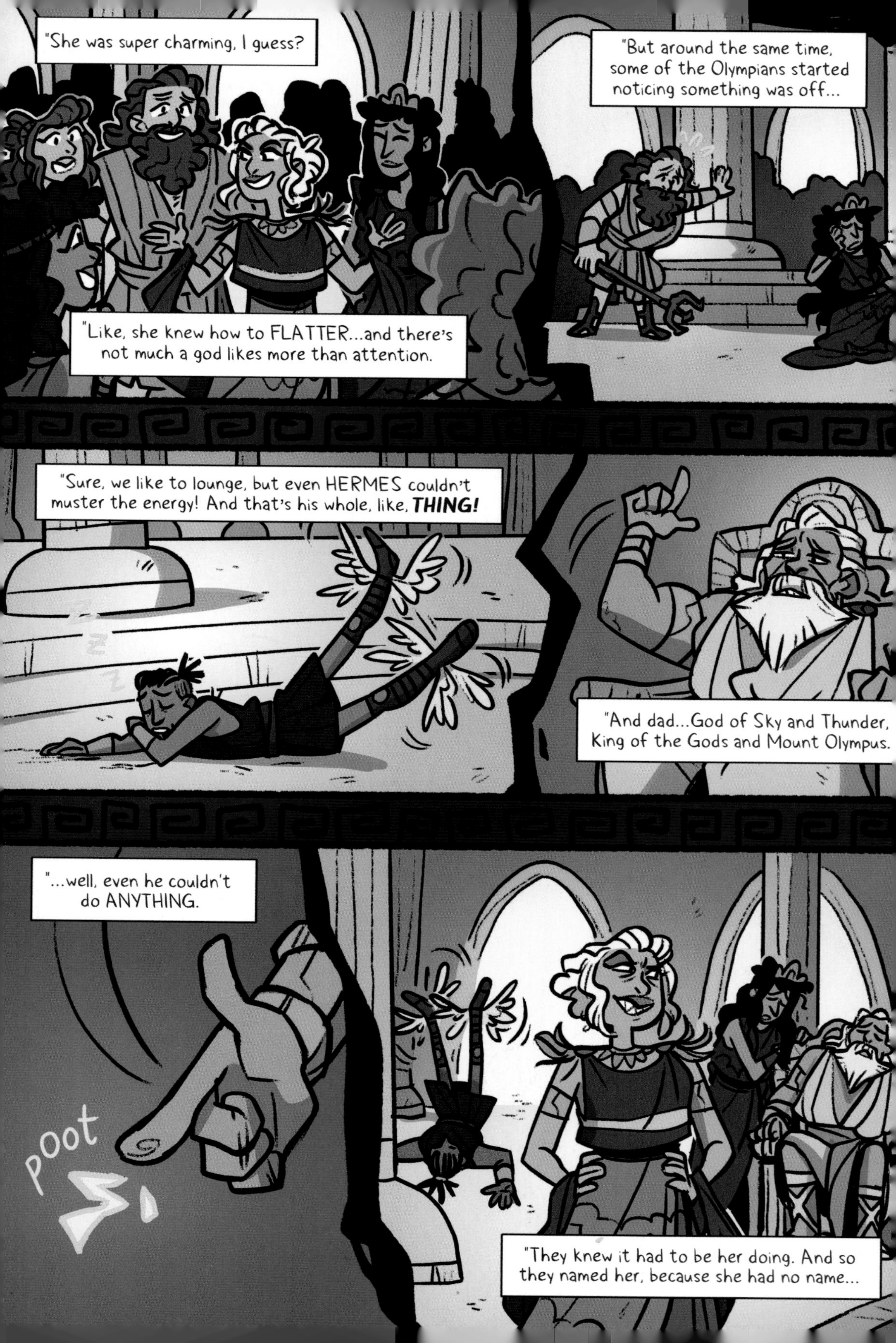
"She was super charming, I guess?
"Like, she knew how to FLATTER...and there's not much a god likes more than attention.
"But around the same time, some of the Olympians started noticing something was off...
"Sure, we like to lounge, but even HERMES couldn't muster the energy! And that's his whole, like, **THING!**
"And dad...God of Sky and Thunder, King of the Gods and Mount Olympus.
"...well, even he couldn't do ANYTHING.
poot
"They knew it had to be her doing. And so they named her, because she had no name...

"...Tromatikós."

Hey, Tammy Tickles!

...Excuse me?

Isn't that what Diane called you? Tammy Tickles?

Tromatikós.

Troma...Tickles?

Tromatikós.

Am I not saying what you're saying?

Anyway, I wanted to ask you, where ARE we?

I was saying--

And how'd we get here?

Where'd my friends go?

Meep?

I have brought you--

Mrow!

What'd you find, Marigold?

GASP!

"So what was she doing exactly?"

And maybe MORE importantly...how did you STOP her?

Well--

"Uncle Hades finally came around Mt. Olympus one day to see why no one was answering his texts, or whatever. He didn't leave the underworld much and hadn't met Tromatikós yet.

"He's the one who finally found her out."

"Solving a problem without their vast, va[st]
VAST amounts of power wasn't someth[ing]
my family had ever had to DEAL with bef[ore.]

"(Being a powerful deity
is usually awesome, natch.)

"She had been feasting on the energy of the gods.

"They were stumped. And so they did
something they never did before or since.

"And when I say everyone...

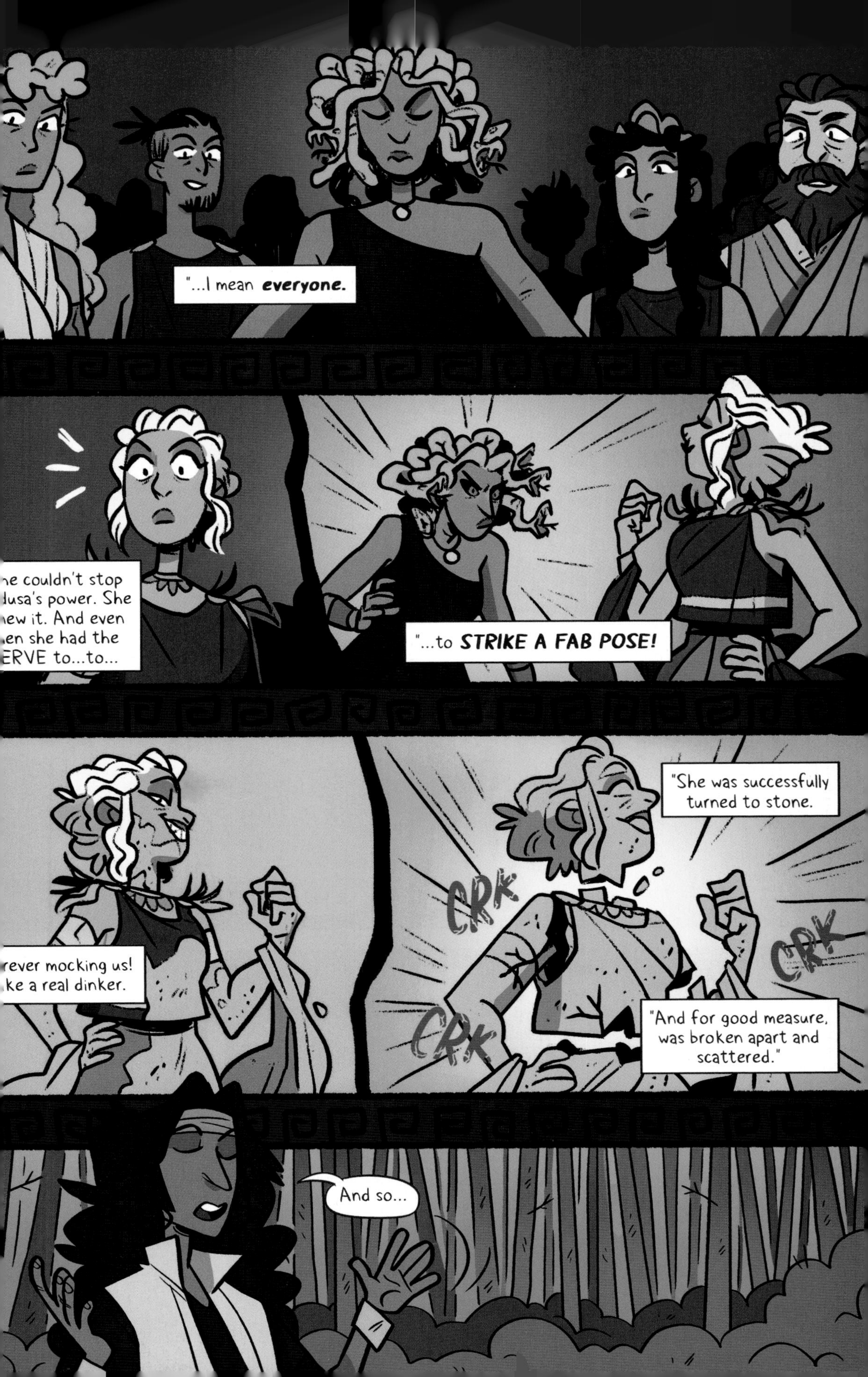
"...I mean everyone.
he couldn't stop
dusa's power. She
new it. And even
en she had the
ERVE to...to...
"...to STRIKE A FAB POSE!
rever mocking us!
ke a real dinker.
"She was successfully
turned to stone.
CRK
CRK
CRK
"And for good measure,
was broken apart and
scattered."
And so...

...How you ever FOUND her, or WHY YOU PUT HER BACK TOGETHER is a mystery to me!

We had a map! And c'mon, we didn't expect her to **COME ALIVE AND BE SUPER DUPER ORIGINAL EVIL!**

I MUST REITERATE THAT I SUPPOSE WE SHOULD HAVE EXPECTED SOMETHING... but not an evil monster!

Wait, a map?

Yeah, actually, Barney, you said you found it.

That map we found in Apollo's room? THAT'S the map you used?

nyah nyah!

She must have used the last of her energy to create it! We had no idea...

And OF COURSE my horrible brother would find it and keep it in his PIG STY OF A ROOM!

OKAY! OKAY!

It's time to focus...

WHERE IS SHE **NOW?!**

Is she going to EAT her!? We have to DO something!

OH, LORD I ALMOST FORGOT-- SHE HAS RIPLEY!

No offense...but humans are a super weak food source for her. Like eating half a peanut! I have no idea why she'd take Ripley!

Some offense.

She also took Marigold...

Yeah, but she's just one little kitten, a MAGIC kitten sure, but--

You don't think--

OH, CRUD! All that stuff we told her!

What "stuff"?

We mayyyy have mentioned the time Ripley had control of all that Ultimate...Supreme Godly Power.

IT WAS ONLY FOR, LIKE, FORTY SECONDS! She doesn't even still HAVE it!

But Trauma lady doesn't know that!

Okay okay okay, WE HAVE TO FIND THEM! DIANE!

I don't KNOW, okay?! I AM NOT IN CHARGE OF KEEPIN TABS ON THE ENTIF DEITY-ADJACENT COMMUNUTY!

Scouts!

Scout Leader Ned? What are you doing here?

Jasmin--

Jen.

--was saying somethin about a vanished scou when Nathan here--

Ned.

--came rushing over asking to speak with young Barney!

Something's happened over at the Scouting Lads campsite...

"...Something AWFUL."

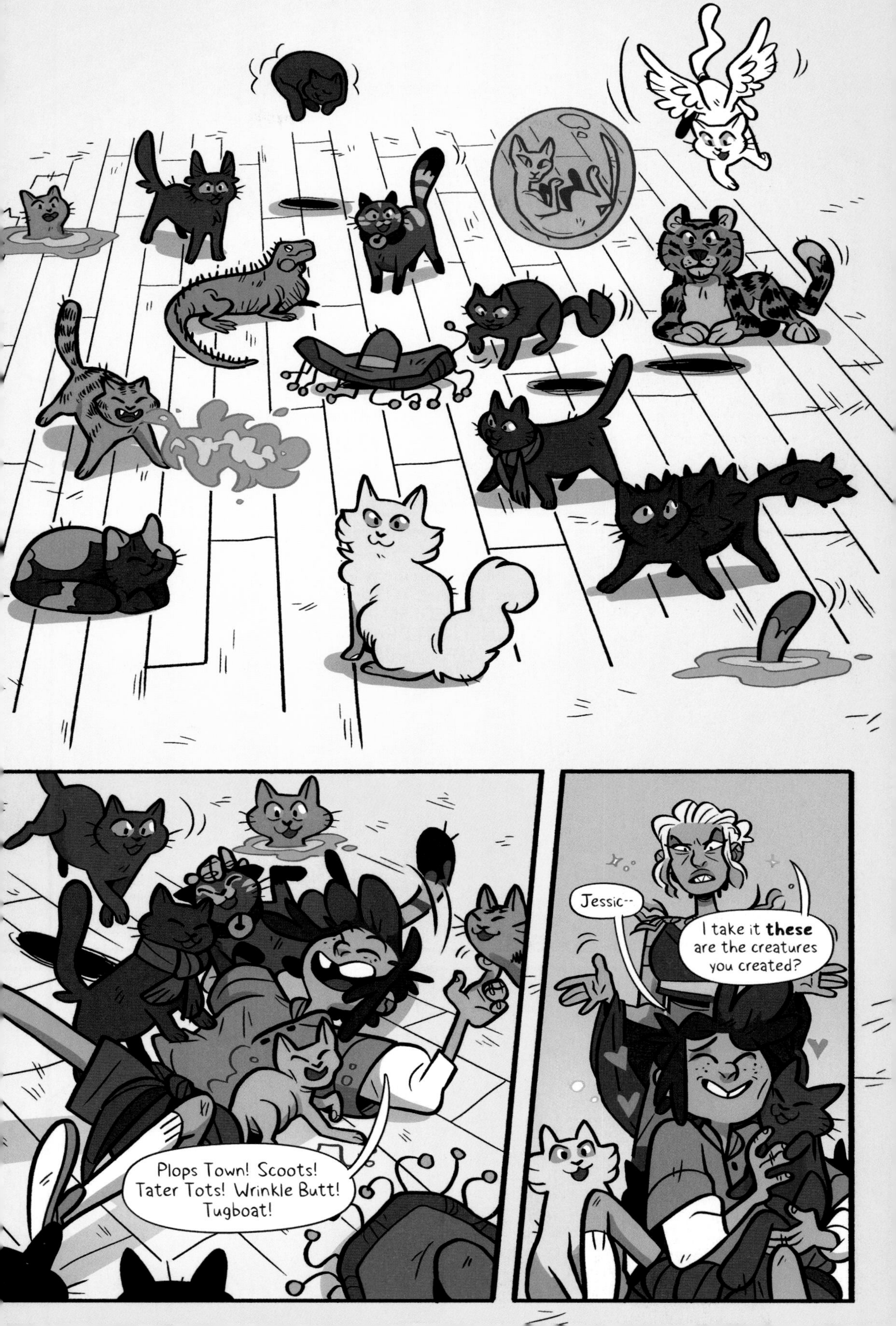
Plops Town! Scoots!
Tater Tots! Wrinkle Butt!
Tugboat!
Jessic--
I take it **these** are the creatures you created?

This is Jessica, Spot, Peanut, Beyoncé, Mr. Chips, Mo-Mo...

Captain Battleship Dangerblast--

What are you doing.

I'm introducing you!

I do not require your names. REVEAL TO ME THE UNLIMITED COSMIC POWER YOU USED TO CREATE ALL THESE CREATURES AND...

sigh

...that...hat.

You want to see their powers?! This'll be fun!

Kitties! Here, kitties! I have crinkles!

Krnk Krck ckl

Here, kitties!

krnk Krck ckl

"And then there was a great big 'POOF!' and they were gone!"

Every single kitten...so I rushed over to see if the same thing happened to Marigold...

...Sorry, Barney...

And Diane, this "Tromatikós" person is responsible?

...Yes.

Hm.

WELP! You scouts hang tight and we'll get this sorted out in a jiffy!

But Rosie--

Let us--

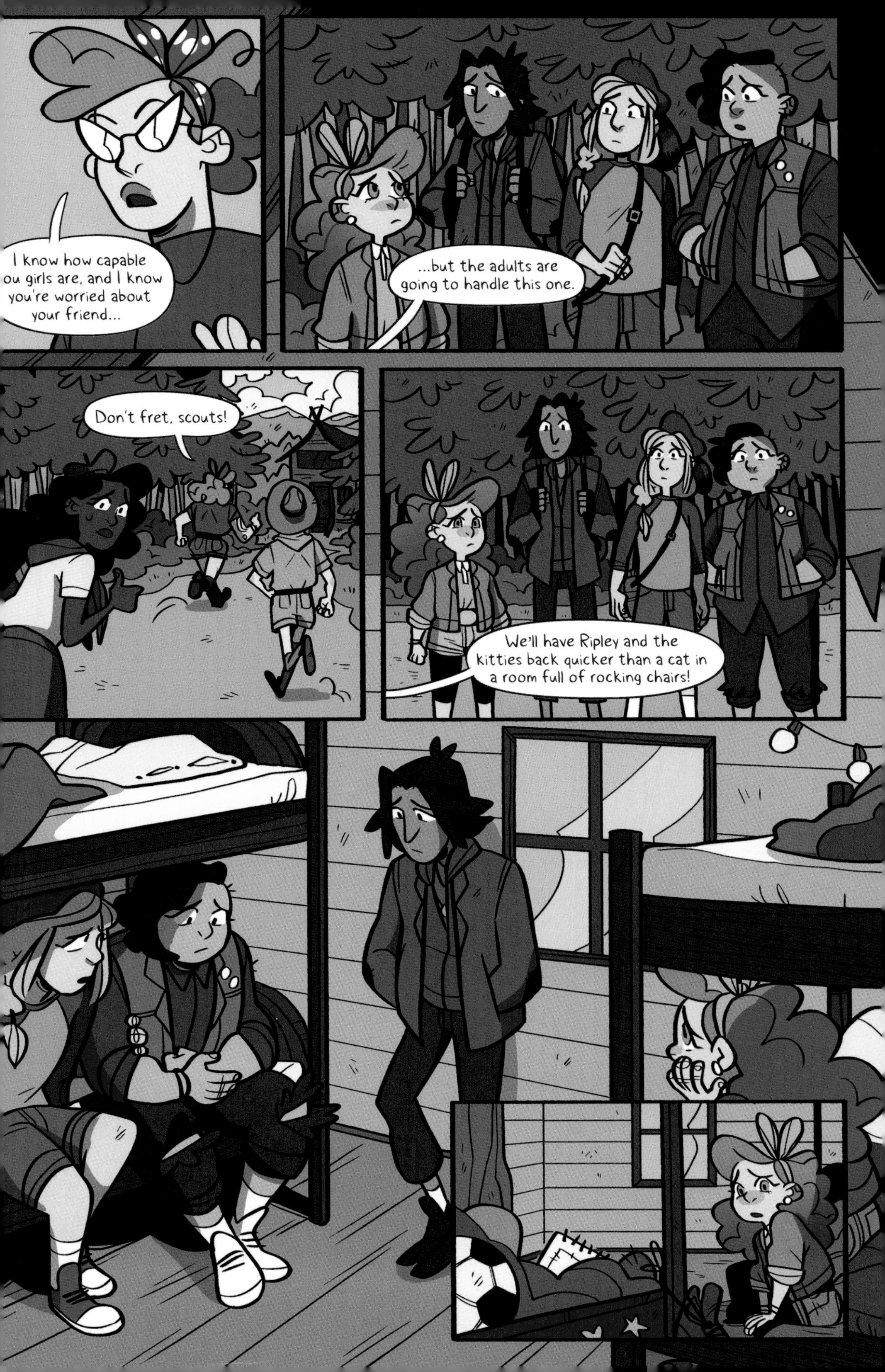
I know how capable ou girls are, and I know you're worried about your friend...
...but the adults are going to handle this one.
Don't fret, scouts!
We'll have Ripley and the kitties back quicker than a cat in a room full of rocking chairs!

ARGH!

tap *tap* *tap*

I CAN'T TAKE THIS! IT'S BEEN HOURS!

...Twenty minutes...

Look girls, I know this is dangerous. I know Rosie told us to leave this to her.

And we all trust Rosie, it's ROSIE for Pauli Murray's sake! But...but...

But...

...it's RIPLEY.

sigh

Diane!

You're all so... NOBLE and junk. It's exhausting.

What do you WANT?

Are you here to help?

No.

ARRGH! Now is NOT the time to be SNOBBY-MODE DIANE!

NO. Like, I can't! I REALLY can't! Like, physically. As in, no one in the Greek Pantheon could!

Zeus placed a SEAL on all of us... even Medusa and her family. Our powers would literally STOP WORKING around Tromatikós. If we can't access our powers...then neither could she, to drain them.

I LITERALLY can't help.

Seems convenient for you...

She's telling the truth.

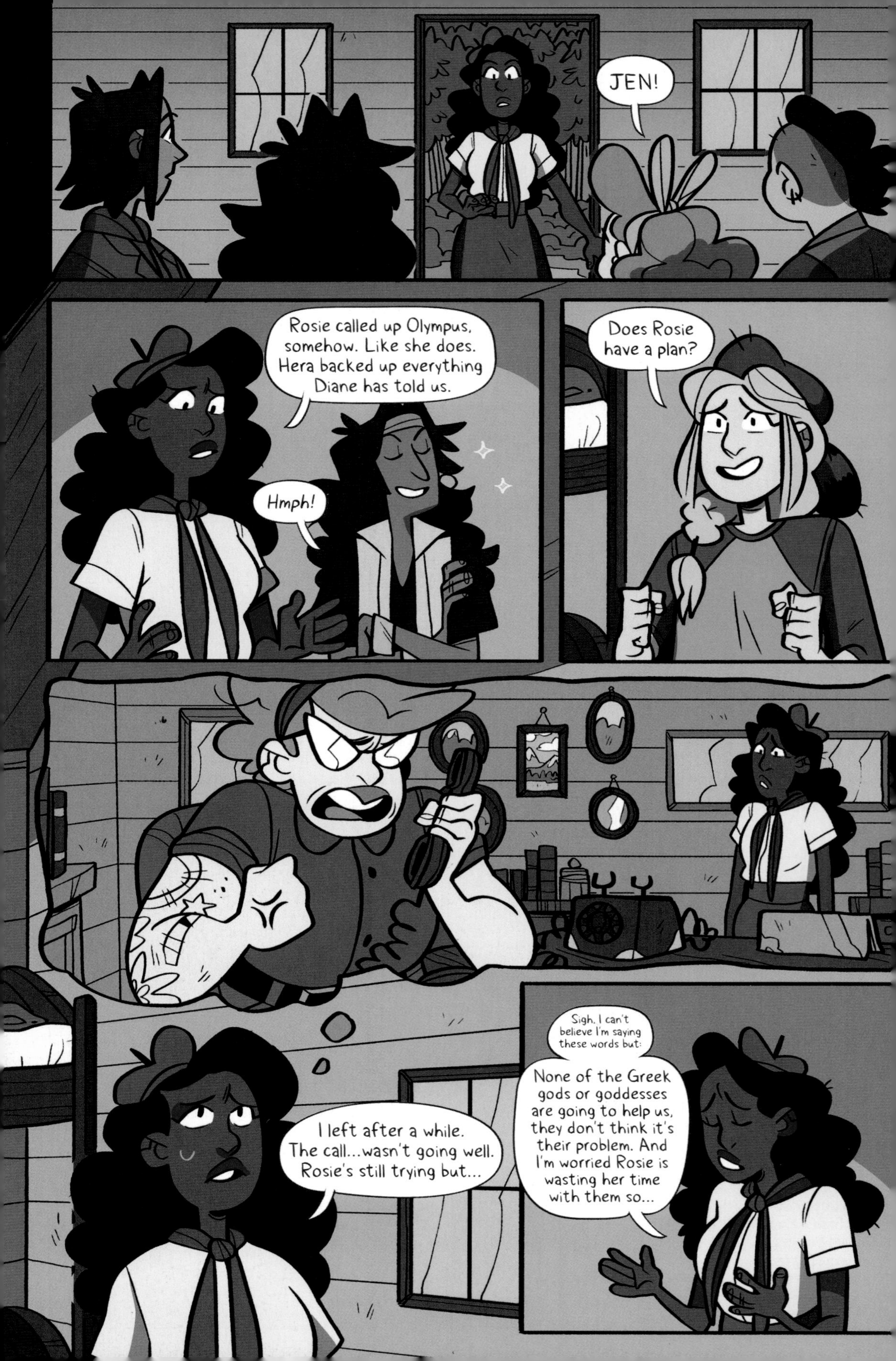
JEN!
Rosie called up Olympus, somehow. Like she does. Hera backed up everything Diane has told us.
Hmph!
Does Rosie have a plan?
I left after a while. The call...wasn't going well. Rosie's still trying but...
Sigh. I can't believe I'm saying these words but:
None of the Greek gods or goddesses are going to help us, they don't think it's their problem. And I'm worried Rosie is wasting her time with them so...

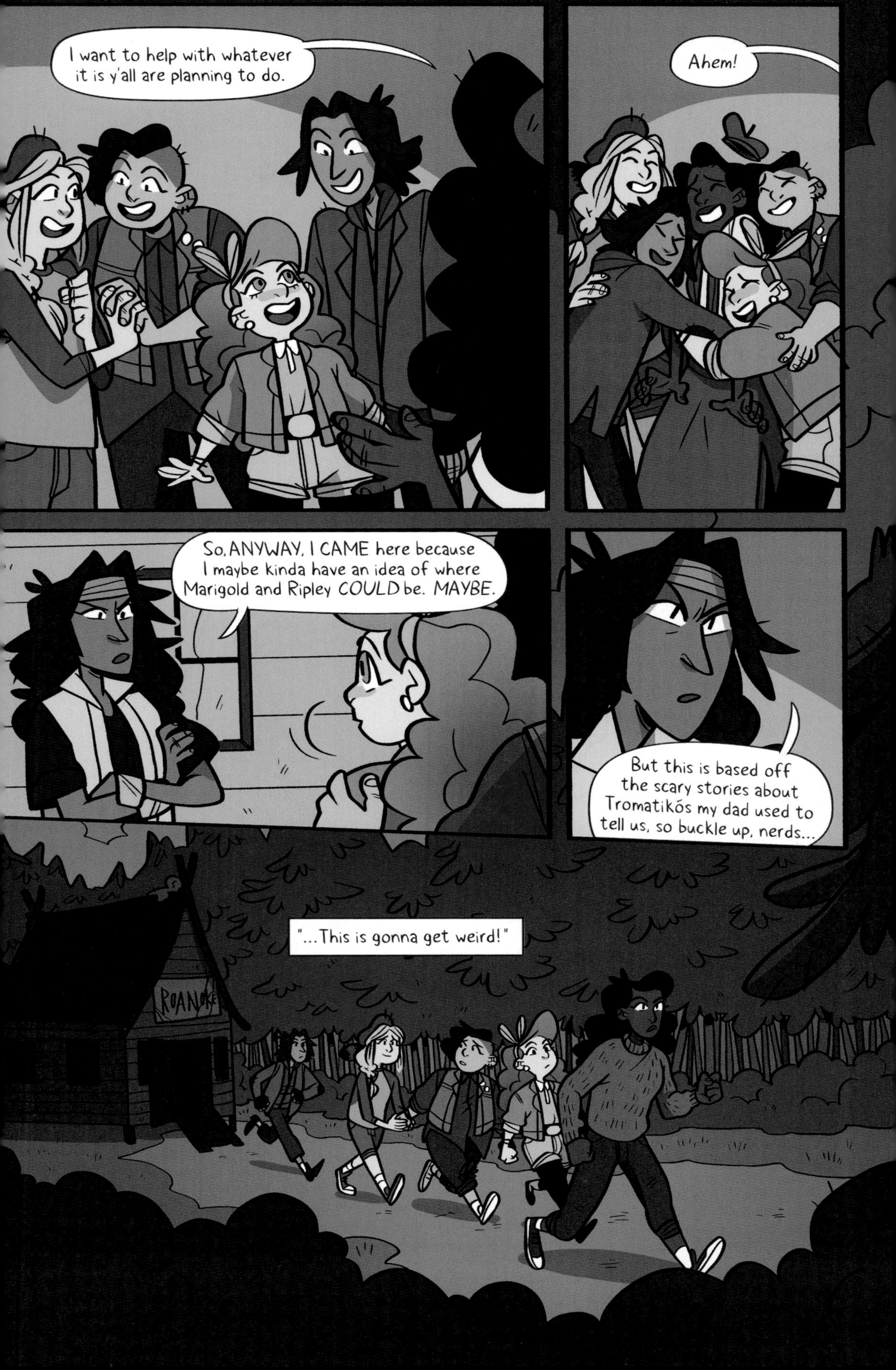
I want to help with whatever it is y'all are planning to do.
Ahem!
So, ANYWAY, I CAME here because I maybe kinda have an idea of where Marigold and Ripley COULD be. MAYBE.
But this is based off the scary stories about Tromatikós my dad used to tell us, so buckle up, nerds...
"...This is gonna get weird!"
ROANOKE

I am NOT feeling great about this plan...

Do you want to stay behind?

Not at all! I just want to be clear: NOT loving this plan...

Noted.

We can DO this...

For Ripley.

"For Ripley."

will co

The
It help
appearan
dress fo
Further
Lumber
to have
part in
Thiskw
Hardc
have
them

The
yellow,
emb
the w
choose
slacks,
made o
out-of-do
green bere
the colla
Shoes ma
heels, roun
socks shou
the uniform. Ne
belong with a Lumberjane uniform.

THE UNIFORM

hould be worn at camp
vents when Lumberjanes
may also be worn at other
ions. It should be worn as a
the uniform dress with
rect shoes, and stocking or
ut grows her uniform or
ther Lumberjane.
a she has
her
her

HOW TO WEAR THE UNIFORM

To look well in a uniform demands first of
uniform be kept in good condition—clean
pressed. See that the skirt is the right length for your own
height and build, that the belt is adjusted to your waist,
that your shoes and stockings are in keeping with the
uniform, that you watch your posture and carry yourself
with dignity and grace. If the beret is removed indoors,
be sure that your hair is neat and kept in place with an
inconspicuous clip or ribbon. When you wear a
Lumberjane uniform you are identified as a member of
this organization and you should be doubly careful to
conduct yourself in a way that will show everyone that
courtesy and thoughtfulness are part of being a
Lumberjane. People are likely to judge a whole nation by
the selfishness of a few individuals, to criticize a whole
family because of the misconduct of one member, and to
feel unkindly toward an organization because of the

The unifor
helps to cre
in a group.
active life th
another bond
future, and pr
in order to b
Lumberjane pr
Penniquiqul Thi
Types, but m
can either bu
materials available at the trading post.

KITTY CHAOS

THE GREATEST DAY OF RIP'S LIFE!

I CAN'T TAKE IT ANYMORE!

LUMBERJANES FIELD MANUAL

CHAPTER
FIFTY-FIVE

Anything yet?

I don't think so?

Diane's directions were... **DISTRESSINGLY** vague...

And CREEPY.

Oh, yeah SUPER creepy.

Well, she IS basing her directions off a scary story her father told her centuries ago, so that makes sense...

BUT it's the only lead we have!

Right!

Mal?

I've been thinking about it...

Tromatikós...she's an energy vampire. A super old, super scary **VAMPIRE** that scares a bunch of very powerful gods, goddesses, and **LITERAL MONSTERS** and we're trying to TRACK HER DOWN!

Because she took our friend...

Hey. If you want to stay--

No. What I'm saying, is that I really, really...

...really, really, REALLY...

...REALLY don't want to go THAT way!

Which means...

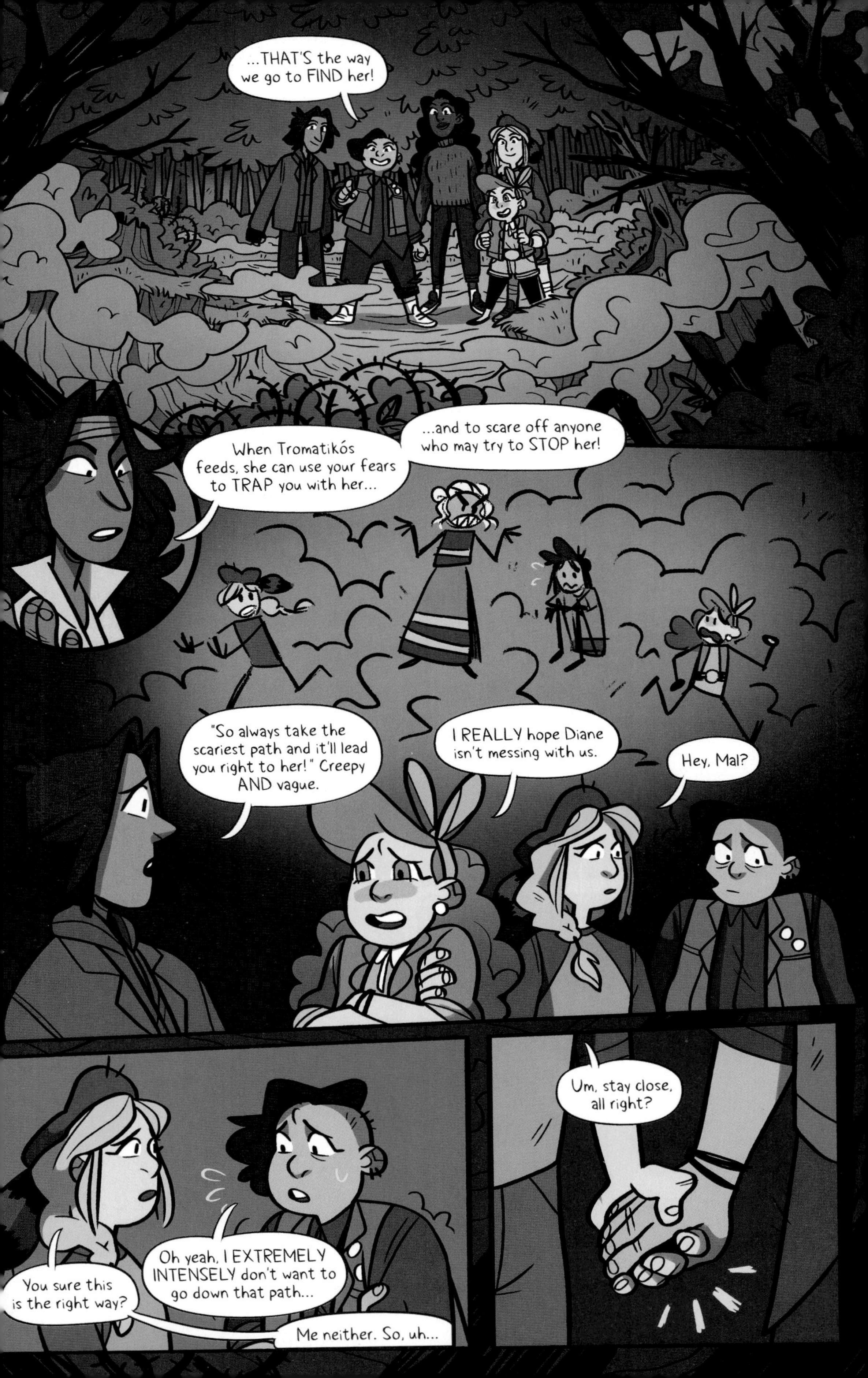

...THAT'S the way we go to FIND her!
When Tromatikós feeds, she can use your fears to TRAP you with her...
...and to scare off anyone who may try to STOP her!
"So always take the scariest path and it'll lead you right to her!" Creepy AND vague.
I REALLY hope Diane isn't messing with us.
Hey, Mal?
You sure this is the right way?
Oh yeah, I EXTREMELY INTENSELY don't want to go down that path...
Me neither. So, uh...
Um, stay close, all right?

LET'S GET THIS VAMPIRE.

Jen, do you think Ripley's holding up alright?

She is.

But if all these super powerful beings are afraid of--

HEY.

Let's not forget who we're talking about!

If there's ANYONE who can outlast an energy sucking nightmare lady...

"...it's Ripley!"

HAHAHA!

TUSSLE

BOUND

POUNCE

LEAP

Haha! That tickles, Scoots!

PHASE

SWOOSH

Whoa!

You are not listening to me AGAIN, human ch--

RIPLEY!

My name's Ripley!

As I have said, I DO NOT REQUIRE YOUR NAME, HUMAN!

I need you to access your unlimited cosmic power so I may--

MROW!

TATER TOTS, NO! BAD KITTY!

FWOOSH!

Oh.

fwwww

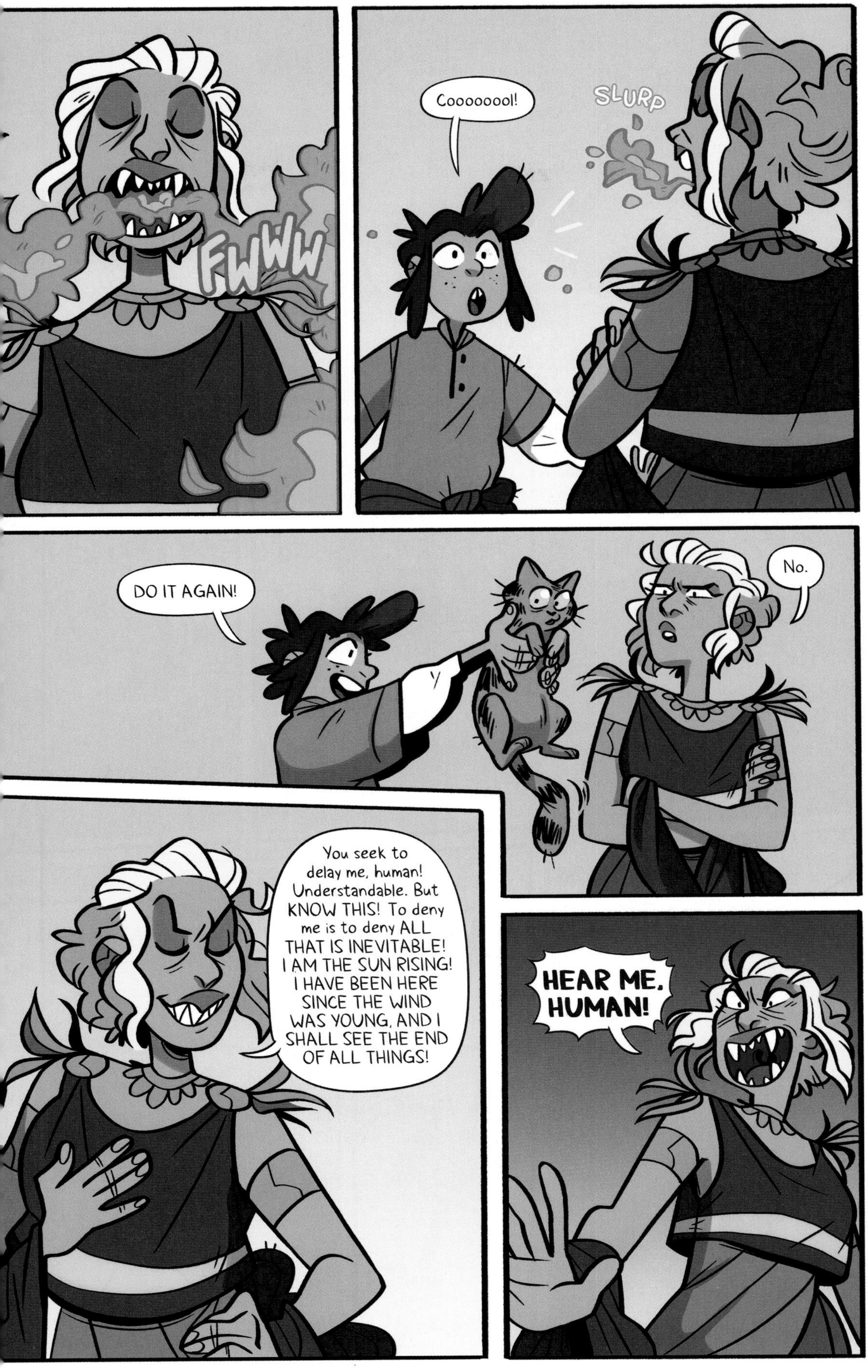
FWWW
Cooooooool!
SLURP
DO IT AGAIN!
No.
You seek to delay me, human! Understandable. But KNOW THIS! To deny me is to deny ALL THAT IS INEVITABLE! I AM THE SUN RISING! I HAVE BEEN HERE SINCE THE WIND WAS YOUNG, AND I SHALL SEE THE END OF ALL THINGS!
HEAR ME, HUMAN!

Oh, curse the gods, NOW where has it gone?

Human! I am unaccustomed to being IGNORED. Stop it.

Sorry, Tickles! What were you saying about the sun? I saw all your awesome stuff and got distracted!

We even like the same kind of candy!

I do not have "candy."

Wait, you FOUND these things here?

It's just like under my bunk, except you've got all these great cat toys! You should have just SAID you wanted to play!

Here!

WATCH THIS!

See? They like to use their powers when they play! Or when you give them scritches!

This is not...NORMAL behavior for a kitten?

Nope! I bet these are the most talented kittens in the whole STATE! **NO!** In the whole COUNTRY!

These kittens... delight you...

...hey DISTRACT you...

I see...

Human...gather the kittens.

Weeell...

...they're preeeetty gathered right now.

This will do.

These kittens will not be a satisfying meal, but I need you to FOCUS.

Focus on ME, fear ME, and SHOW ME YOUR POWER!

A *meal?*

Creating this space, bringing you all here...it took a toll on my reserves. And now...

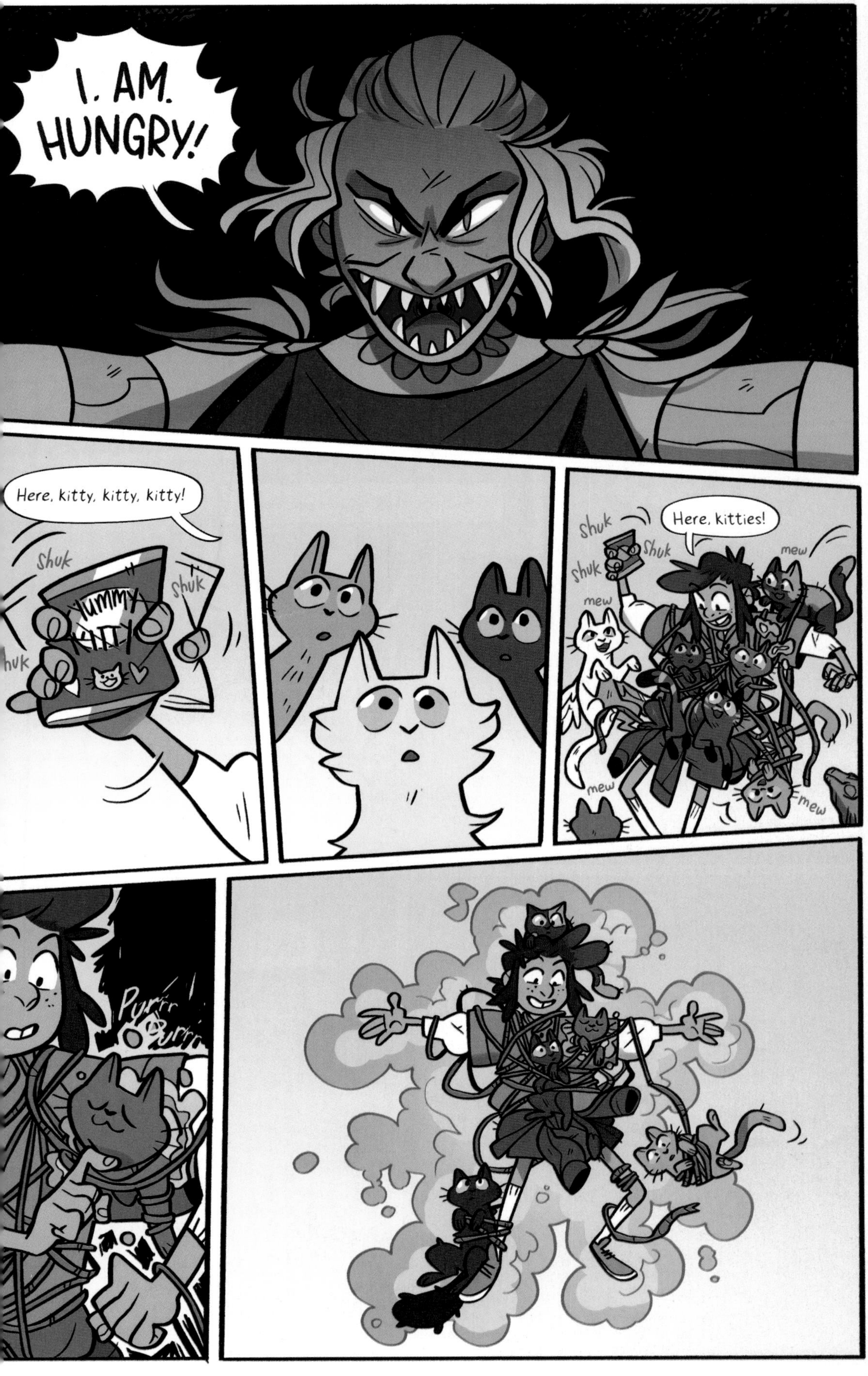
I. AM. HUNGRY!
Here, kitty, kitty, kitty!
shuk
shuk
YUMMY
Here, kitties!
shuk
shuk
shuk
mew
mew
mew
mew
Purrr

Wh--

y

PHASE

Hey!

You may run from me...

"...but not **that which you fear!**"

Is it just me, or did things just get a whole lot spookier?

And a whole lot...grayer?

That's, uh, a GOOD thing, right? It means we're getting closer? RIGHT?!

GASP!

rustle
rustle

Did anyone see that? There's something in the trees!

I SAW **THAT!**

rustle rustle

It's okay, it's okay! This is just trick to scare us! It means we're on the right path.

Or it could just be real wolves. We ARE wandering around a forest at night.

Not helping, Mal!

Uh, it's definitely not wolves...

Is that...

That's a... movie monster?!

It LITERALLY is! It's got a zipper!

That's not so sc--

Uh, girls?

It's not the only one.

HSSSSSSSSSS

Okay, THAT'S not a special effect!

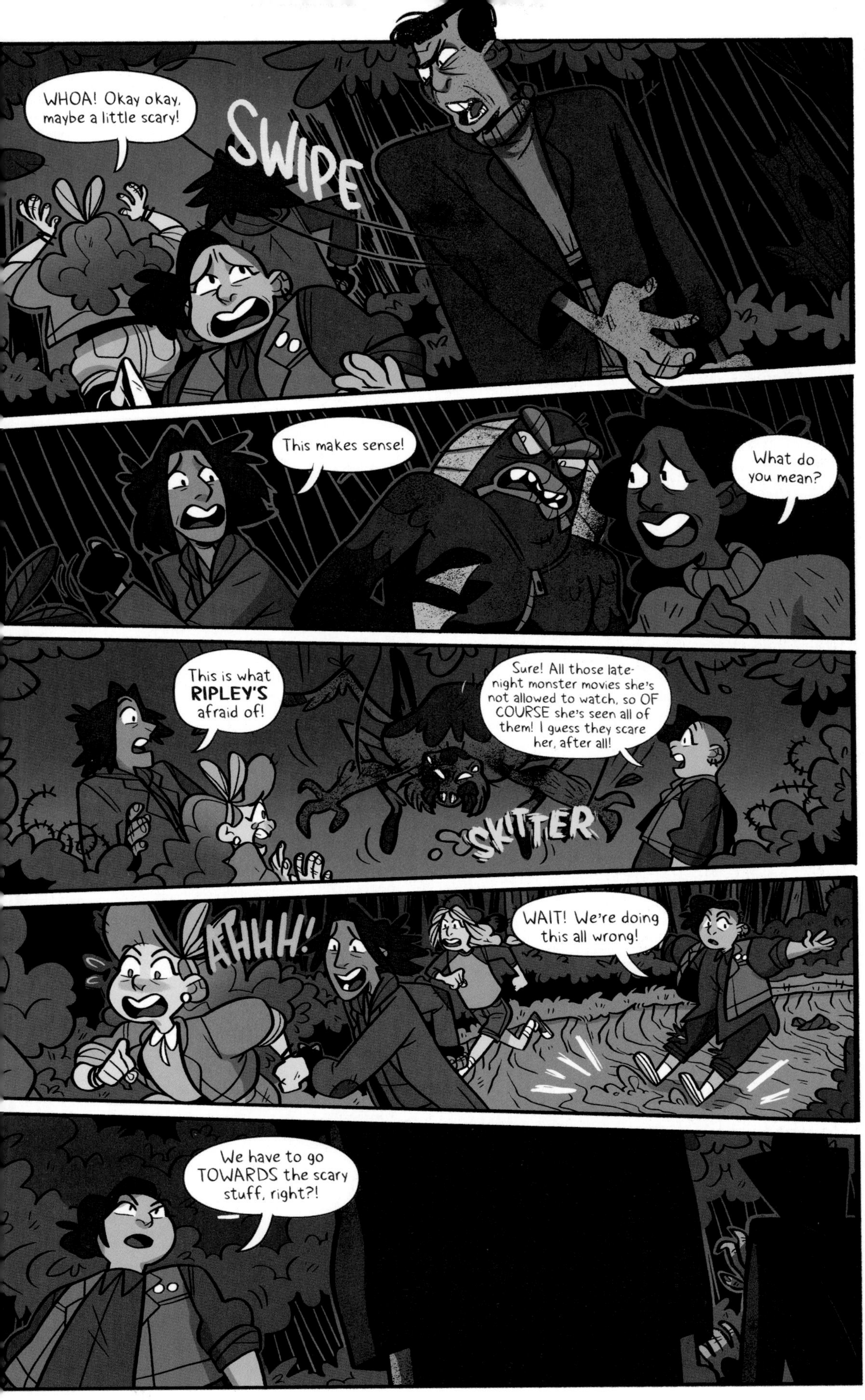
WHOA! Okay okay, maybe a little scary!
SWIPE
This makes sense!
What do you mean?
This is what RIPLEY'S afraid of!
Sure! All those late-night monster movies she's not allowed to watch, so OF COURSE she's seen all of them! I guess they scare her, after all!
SKITTER
AHHH!
WAIT! We're doing this all wrong!
We have to go TOWARDS the scary stuff, right?!

RAHHHHH!

AAAAH!

POW!

YAAAAH!

Here, kitties! Treats, kitties!

The monsters aren't real... the monsters aren't real...

shuk shuk shuk

:mew: :mew: :mew: :mew:

The monsters aren't--

BWA!

PLOPS TOWN! NO!

yoink!

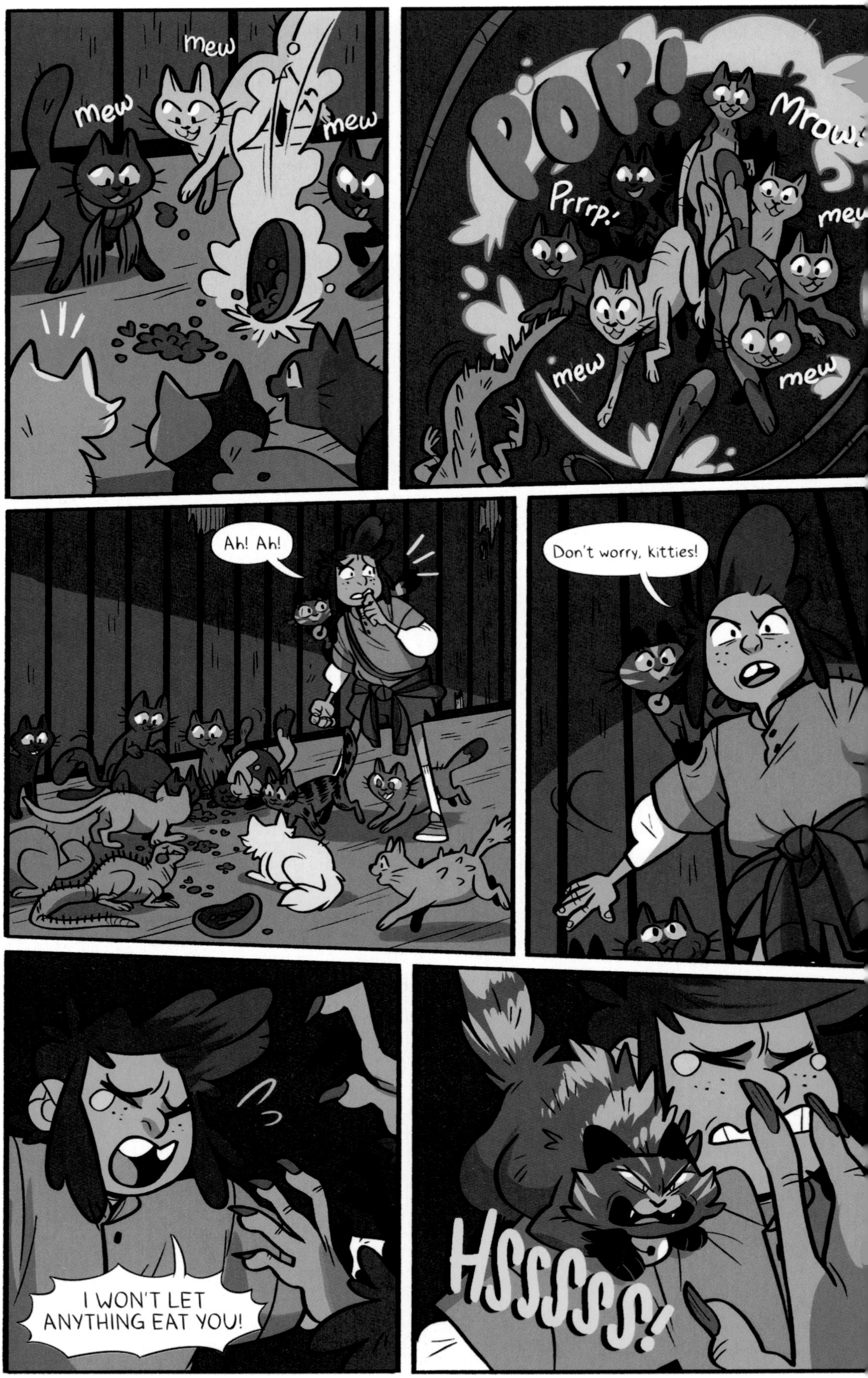

mew
mew
mew
POP!
Mrow!
Prrrp!
mew
mew
mew
Ah! Ah!
Don't worry, kitties!
I WON'T LET ANYTHING EAT YOU!
HSSSSS!

mmrrRROOOW!

BOOF!

PURRRR
PURRRR

Thanks, Marigold!

PAF!

WHAT WAS THAT?!

You didn't lift a finger against your greatest fear!

Surely with your power, you could have easily dealt with them!

I am HUNGRY.

I'll share my cand--

SMK!

Show me your POWER!

brrrrrr

My power? I don't have it anymore.

...What.

Yeah! I made four wishes! For Bubbles to have a funny hat, for Apollo and Artemis to never be able to hurt anyone ever again, for everyone to have a kitten...

...and for the power to be gone forever!

whomp whomp!

If yours isn't the power I've been sensing this whole time...where is it coming from?

I don't know! There's a lot of weird magic stuff here!

"Here"?

Yeah! Camp... the forest...

Yes, of course! It was never a person I was seeking...but a place!

Sooo...you're not going to eat the kittens anymore, right?

No, no, I have no need.

phew

I will devour this whole PLACE!

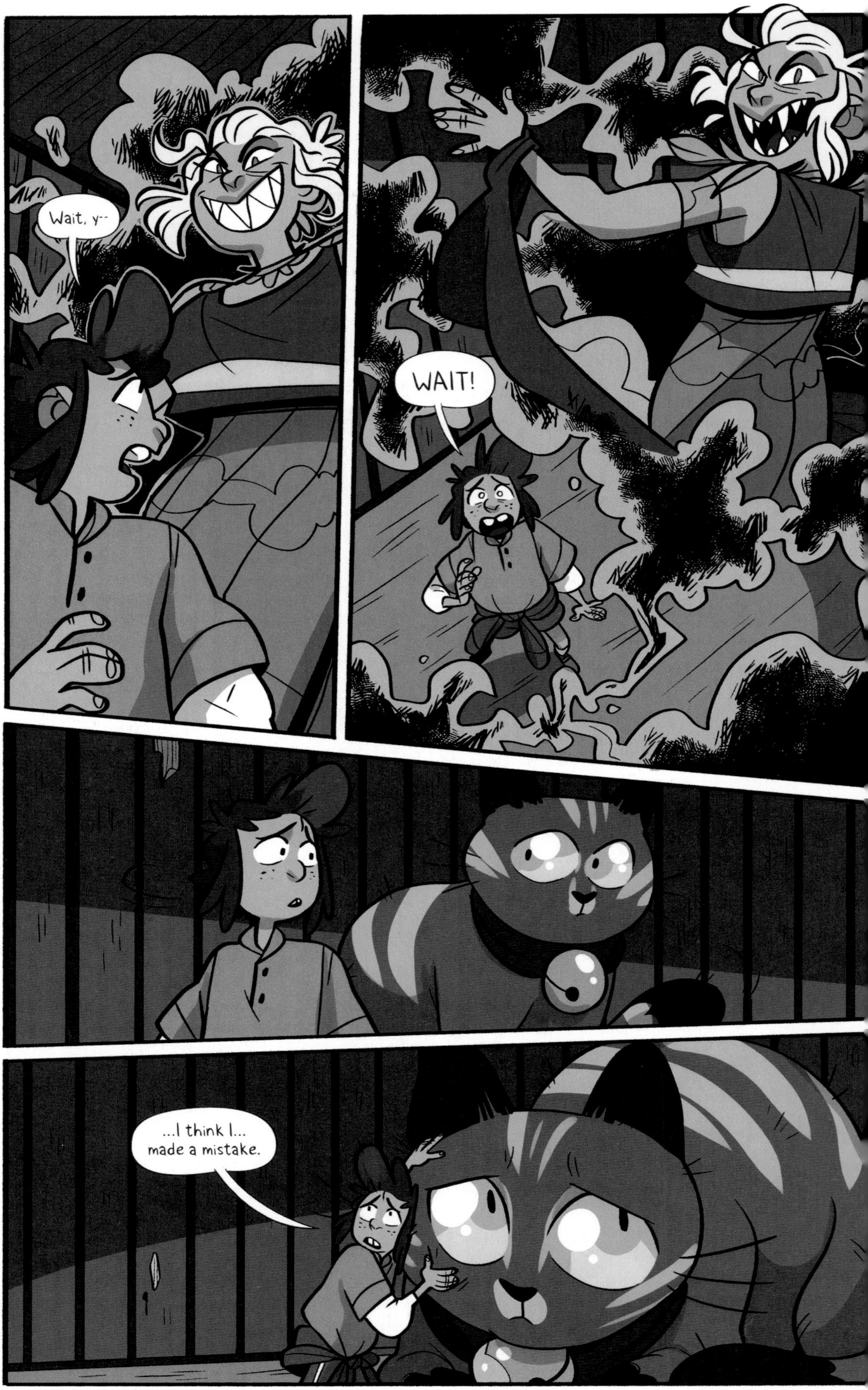

Wait, y--
WAIT!
...I think I...
made a mistake.

will co
The u
It help   hould be worn at camp
appearan   events when Lumberjanes
dress f   may also be worn at other
Further   ions. It should be worn as a
Lumber   the uniform dress with
to have   rrect shoes, and stocking or
part in
Thiskv   out grows her uniform or
Hardc   her Lumberjane.
have   a she has
them   her
                                                             her

The
yellow, short sl
emb
the w
choose
slacks,
made o
out-of-do
green bere
the colla
Shoes may b
heels, round
socks should   with the shoes or wit
the uniform. Ne   es, bracelets, or other jewelry do
belong with a Lumberjane uniform.

HOW TO WEAR THE UNIFORM

To look well in a uniform demands first of
uniform be kept in good condition—clean
pressed. See that the skirt is the right length for your own
height and build, that the belt is adjusted to your waist,
that your shoes and stockings are in keeping with the
uniform, that you watch your posture and carry yourself
with dignity and grace. If the beret is removed indoors,
be sure that your hair is neat and kept in place with an
inconspicuous clip or ribbon. When you wear a
Lumberjane uniform you are identified as a member of
this organization and you should be doubly careful to
conduct yourself in a way that will show everyone that
courtesy and thoughtfulness are part of being a
Lumberjane. People are likely to judge a whole nation by
the selfishness of a few individuals, to criticize a whole
family because of the misconduct of one member, and to
feel unkindly toward an organization because of the

The unifor
helps to cre
in a group.
active life th
another bond
future, and pr
in order to b
Lumberjane pr
Penniquiqul Thi   re Lady
Types, but m   es will wish to have one. They
can either b   e uniform, or make it themselves from
materials available at the trading post.

LUMBERJANES FIELD MANUAL

CHAPTER
FIFTY-SIX

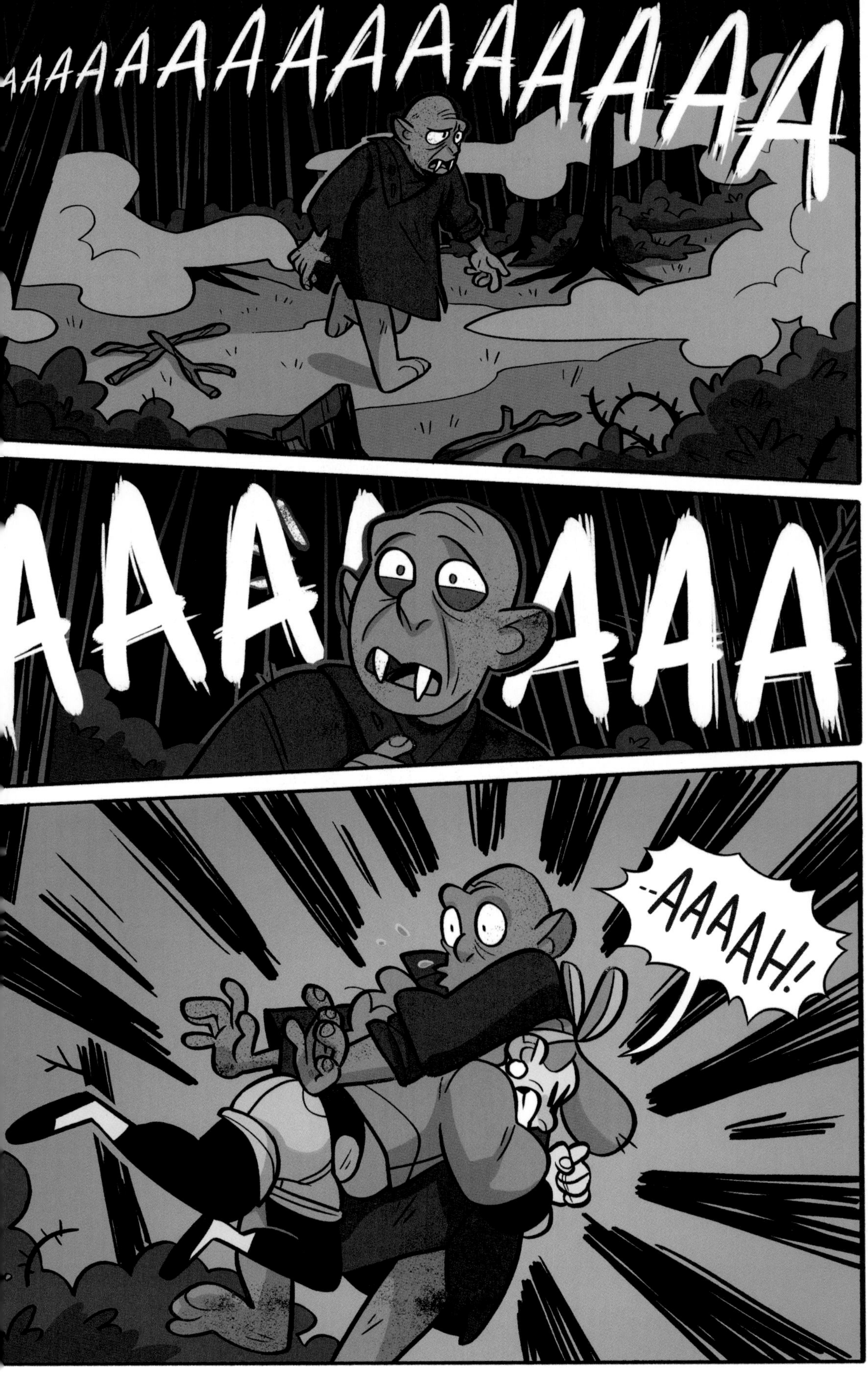
AAAAAAAAAAAAAAA
AAA AAA
--AAAAAH!

ARGH!

-huff-

-huff-

-huff-

THESE THINGS ARE RELENTLESS!

SO AM I!

I've got it by its puppet strings!

STOMP

stomp

stomp

stomp

RRRAAAH

How many of these late-night monster movie marathons did Ripley WATCH?!

ALL of them...

...and all the sequels...

sigh

Just remember, girls...

...on the other side of these BARGAIN BASEMENT BOZOS, our friend is waiting for us!

The only thing to be afraid of 'round here is ME!

You tired?

I could do this all day!

shkrsh krsh

Do you hear that?

Krsh krsh KRSH

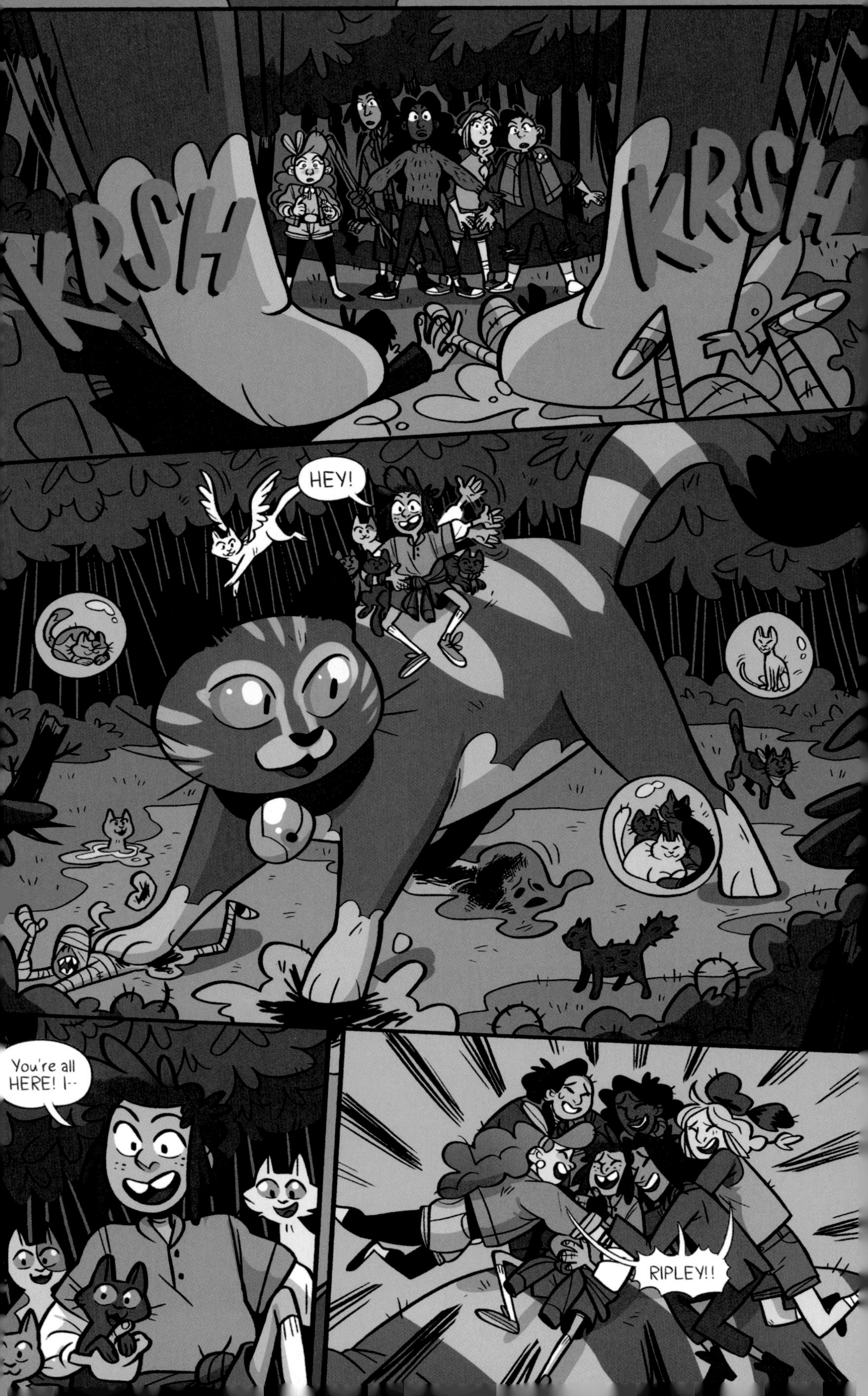
KRSH
KRSH
HEY!
You're all HERE! I--
RIPLEY!!

C'mon, guys! Stuff is still happening!

We know! We tackled THE MONSTERS OF YOUR INNERMOST NIGHTMARES to get here!

Are you okay?

How'd you get away from her?

Where is she now?

That's what I--

HANDS UP TOP!

That means stop!

We can get all caught up BACK at camp, Rosie need to know Ripley's safe and--

But we're **NOT** safe! Tickles is planning something real bad and--

Tickles?

You're back with us. You're safe. We're going to go back and tell Rosie everything right now!

But she's SO DANGEROUS--

That's all the more reason to go back to camp!

"Tromatikós is r your responsibili

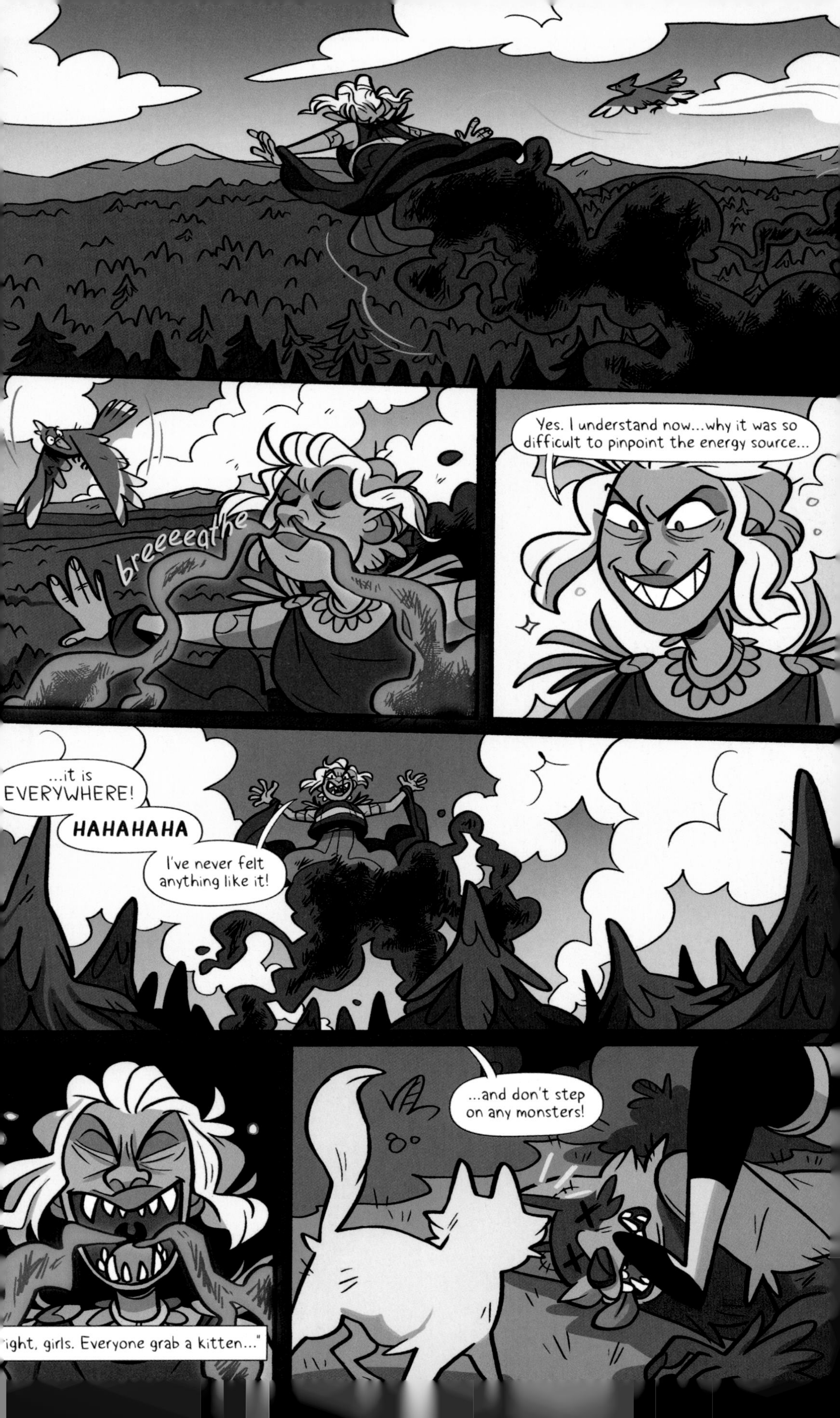
breeeeathe
Yes. I understand now...why it was so difficult to pinpoint the energy source...
...it is EVERYWHERE!
HAHAHAHA
I've never felt anything like it!
'ight, girls. Everyone grab a kitten..."
...and don't step on any monsters!

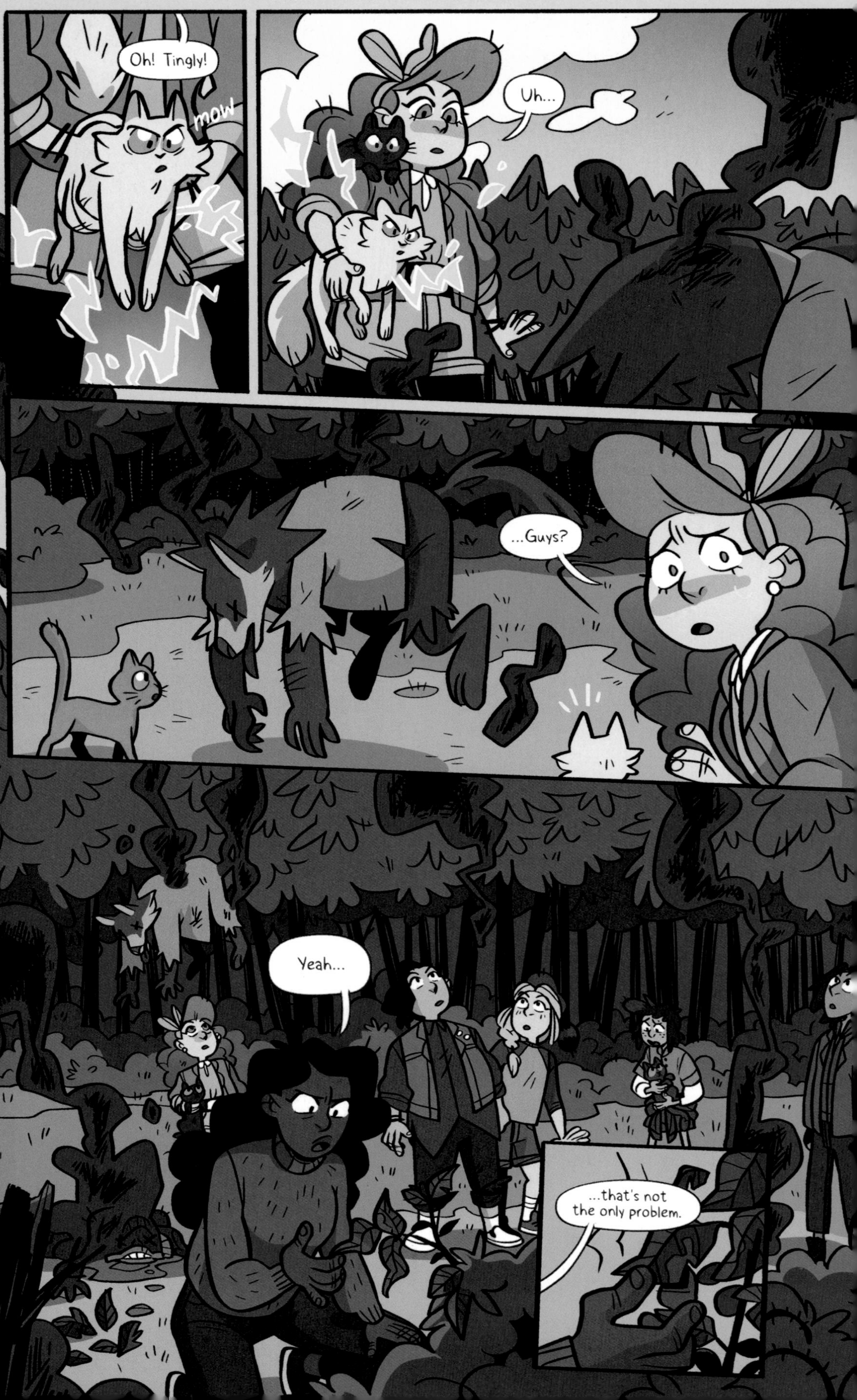
Oh! Tingly!
mow
Uh...
...Guys?
Yeah...
...that's not the only problem.

...Plops Town
...Peanut...
Mr. Chips...

Jen, maybe we SHOULD stay and do something.

This is looking pretty serious.

What if Rosie doesn't have a plan?

breeeeathe

Girls, I'm sorry, but we're NOT taking care of this ourselves! We're going back to camp, NOW!

We can't!

Huh?

WE'RE MISSING A KITTEN!

What is this.

meow

I'm sure it's fine. It's probably on its way back home.

But JEN!

We already shouldn't BE out here, Ripley! We got you back, and now it's up to me to bring you all home safely! I'll come back for the kitten **myself** if I have to...

...but all of you are my **FIRST** priority. Do you understand?

I do.

Now, let's GO!

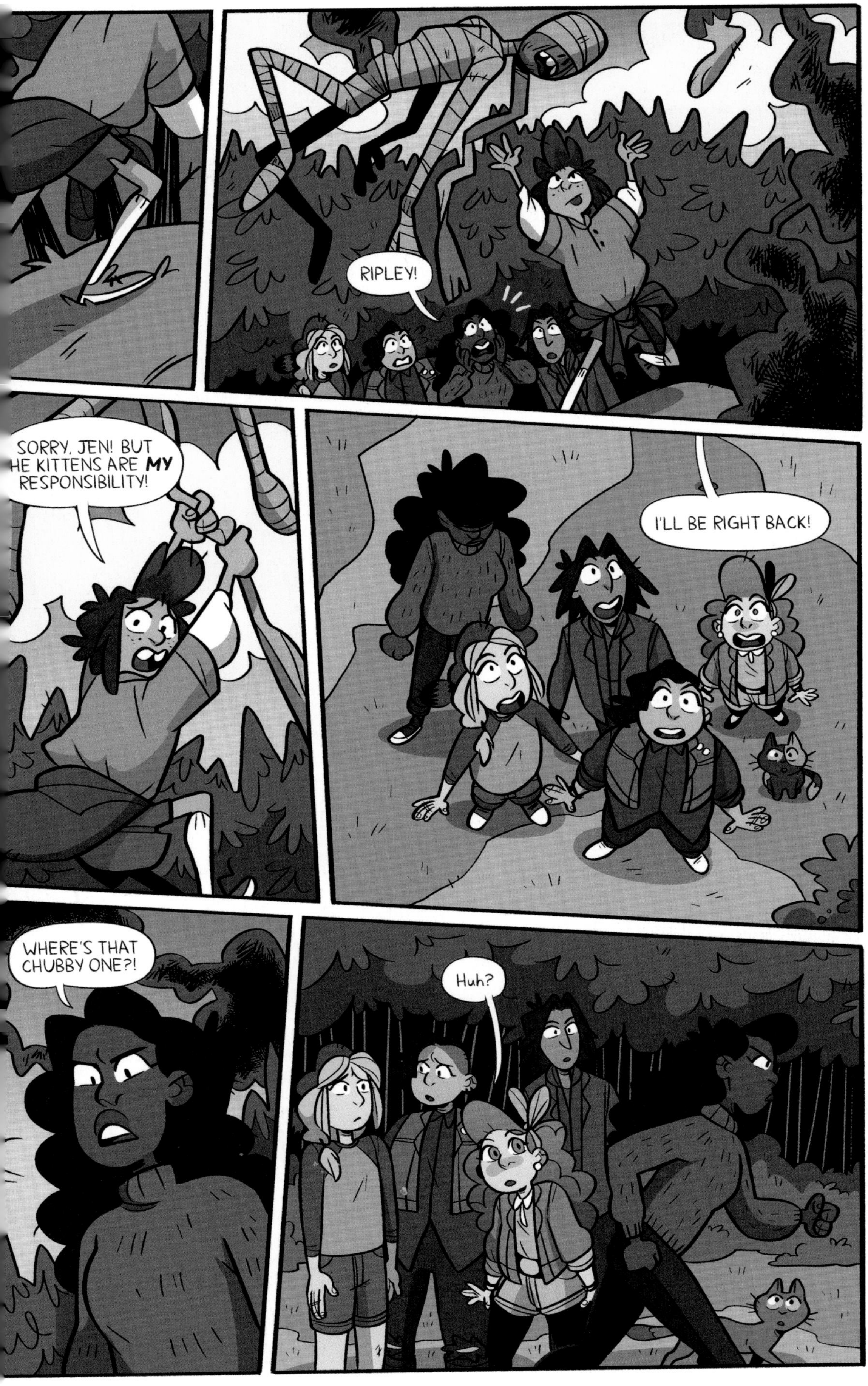
RIPLEY!
SORRY, JEN! BUT
HE KITTENS ARE **MY**
RESPONSIBILITY!
I'LL BE RIGHT BACK!
WHERE'S THAT
CHUBBY ONE?!
Huh?

The little chubby kitten with the scarf? Poopyville? Potty City?

Plops Town.

Ooooh, no.

Nuh-uh. If any of you think you're coming along after the speech I JUST GAVE--

NO TIME TO ARGUE, JEN!

DANGIIIIIIT!

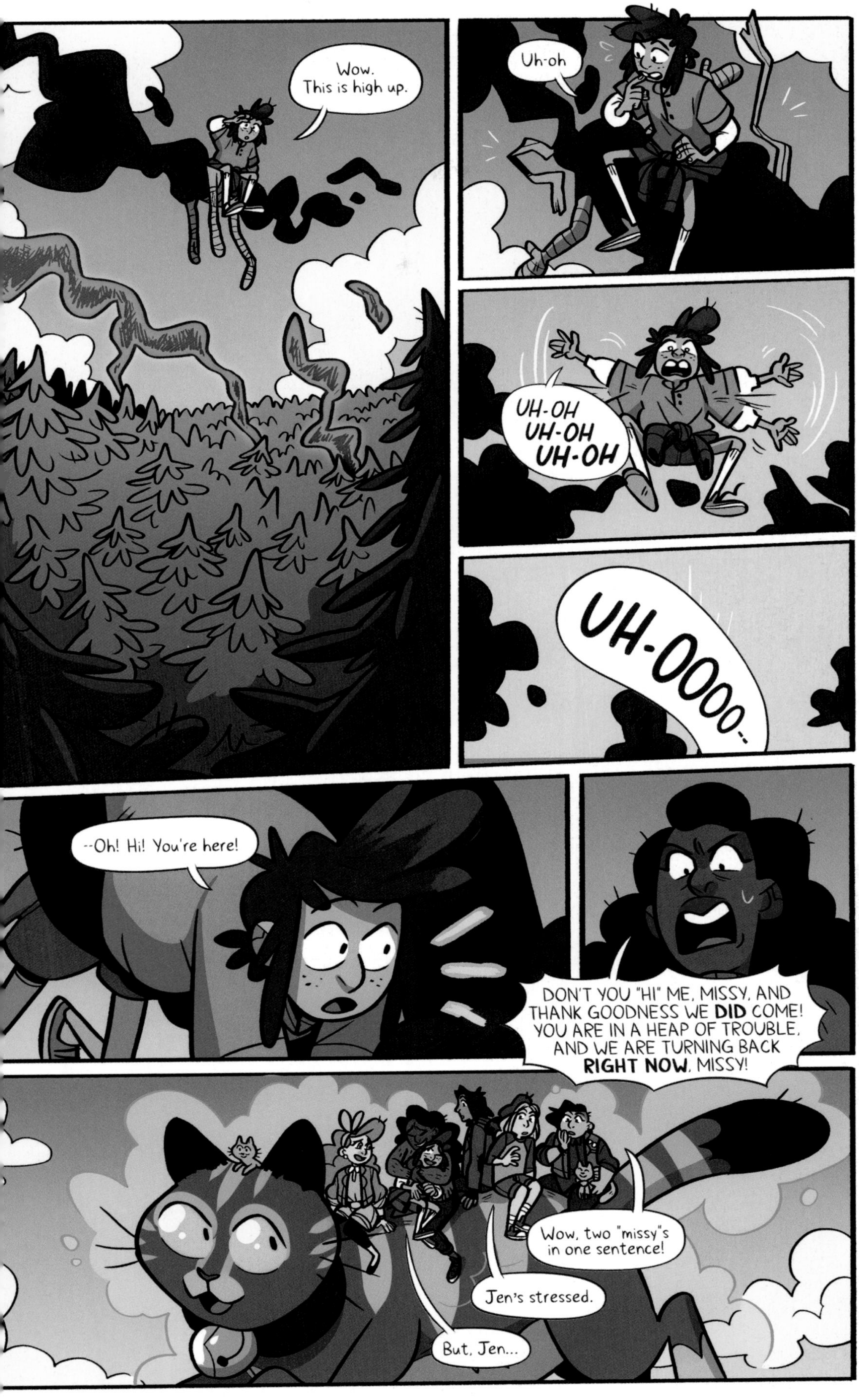
Wow.
This is high up.
Uh-oh
UH-OH
UH-OH
UH-OH
UH-OOOO--
--Oh! Hi! You're here!
DON'T YOU "HI" ME, MISSY, AND THANK GOODNESS WE **DID** COME! YOU ARE IN A HEAP OF TROUBLE, AND WE ARE TURNING BACK **RIGHT NOW**, MISSY!
Wow, two "missy"s in one sentence!
Jen's stressed.
But, Jen...

...we're already here!

You again!

Is this one of your kitten monsters?

meow

Spot!

Don't hurt 'im!

What is...

Spot! Good kitty!

I think I have a plan!

I need you all to be as hyper and distracting as you can. Give it 110%.

The same goes for you.

I would be honored, Jen.

This is the greatest thing anyone's ever asked me to do!

And I've got just what we need!

WHAP!

HEY, TICKLES!

EVER SEEN A BUNCH OF PRE-TEENS ON A SUGAR RUSH...

...AND TWO DOZEN KITTENS PLAY...

...WITH CATNIP?

I know not of what you spe--

MROW

MEW

PRRUP

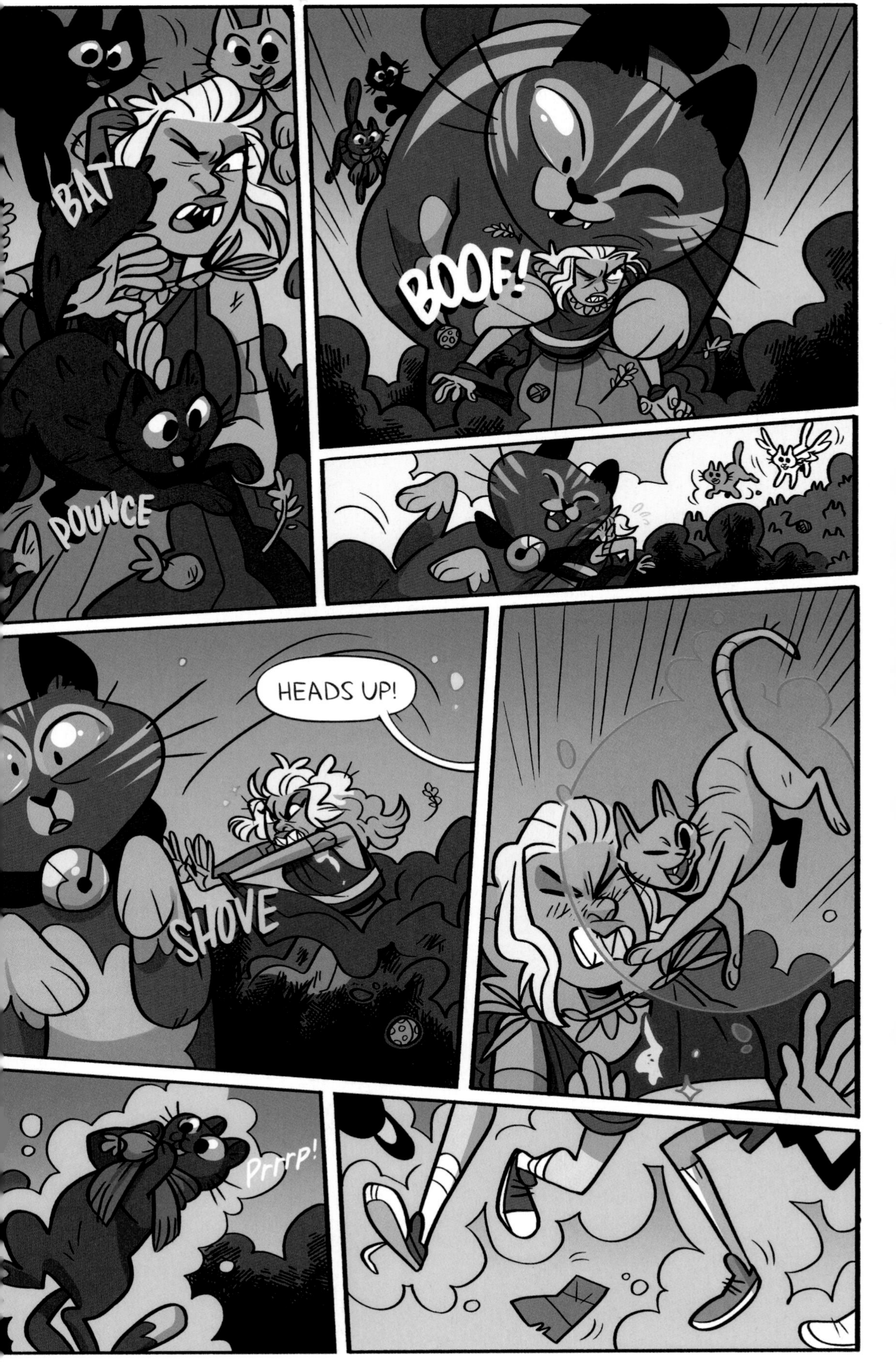
BAT
POUNCE
BOOF!
HEADS UP!
SHOVE
Prrrp!

hee hee

CEASE THIS AT ONC--

WOOOO!

ARGH!

Enough of this.

IT'S TIME!

SENDING PEANUT OVER!

HEAVE!

5 TONS

Purr Purr purr

PAF!

You INSUFFERABLE...

...BRATS! I will DEVOUR every drop of life and power from this place, but FIRST, I will eat YOU ALL, JUST TO STOP YOUR ANNOYIN--

NYAH NYAH! BET YOU WON'T, TICKLES!

My name...